Every Bottle Has a Story

EVERY BOTTLE HAS A STORY

A Wine-Lover's Short Story Collection

JOHN J. MAHONEY

DUBLIN   NEW YORK   MILMAY

John Mahoney can be reached through e-mail at j.mahoney@juno.com

First printing, March 2012

ISBN: 978-1470127985

5 7 9 8 6

To my wife, Joanne.

In Vino Veritas

Contents

Acknowledgements

To the people who have taught me to live better with wine and to those who have shown me that wine is the fundamental symbol of civilization, I owe so much. You've changed my life for the better.

Discussing Champagne with Ed McCarthy, *Wine for Dummies*, sipping simple wines with George Tabor, *Judgment of Paris*, *To Cork or Not To Cork* and *A Toast to Bargain Wines* and learning the Italian wine laws with Sharron McCarthy has increased my knowledge. Having met and talked with Leon Adams, whose *The Wines of America*, or Gerald Asher, whose *On Wine* has been invaluable. Sitting in a wine session with Marian Baldy, whose *The University Wine Course* helps all wine lovers and having traveled and tasted with Monika Elling and Harriet Lembeck, who edits *Grossman's Guide to Wines, Beers and Spirits* helps any wine lover know more. Drinking wine with Kevin Zraly, *Windows on the World Complete Wine Course* and watching him teach about wine, instills the pure passion for wine that you need to truly discover its magic.

Sharing and studying wines with Dionysian Society Tastevin members like Frank Aquilino, Joe Ardito, Carl Brandhorst, Vince Casbarro, Robert Casella, Robin Daplyn, David DeMeo, Anthony Fisher, Richard Gerber, Marion Gorelick, Jerry Gorman, Joe Ingemi, Maynard Johnston, Barry Lawrence, Joe Lertch, Sharon Levine, Pete Mariotti, Archie Mazzoli, Mary Millar, Tad Naprava, Gary Pavlis, Walt Salvadore, Armand Savino, Mike Segarra, Frank

Scarpa, Charles Schaffer and Vince and Susie Winterling have increased my wine knowledge. Doing wine tastings with Dionysians Nick Yankanich, Ben Yang, Bob and Cynthia Walker, Anne Vercelli, Charles Tomasello, Pete Steenland, Christine Skandis, the late Lucio Sorre, Barbara Segarra, Michael Schaefer, Pat Ruster, the late Dave Ricci, Jim Quarella, Gary Pulz, Tony Monfredo, Jan Mitrocsak, Greg Mills, Sheila McHenry, the late Phillip Mazzoni, Murk Lels, Diana Liberto, Larry Levine, Barbara Johnston, Mark Imbesi, Tula Christopoulos, the late Jeff Hondo, Alan Hess, Jim Hemesath, Mike Grass, Lorna Gorman, Glenn Gorman, Don Graham, Cosmo Giovianazzi, Tom Galbiati, Marc Franken, Bill Fennen, Jack Egan, Frank DeCicco, Andrea Daniel, Joe Courter, Tom Castronovo, Frank Calderaro, Joe Broski, Sherman Bruchansky, Valerie Mollick, JB Borreggine, Al Natali, Karen Goetz and Jacqueline Apgar have highlighted wine studies and pointed the way to a civilized society through wine.

Wine professionals like Mark Chandler, Kristin Colasurdo Keating, Michael and David Craig, Michael Mitilla, Owen Altbaum, Marsha Palanci, Arnold Trabb, and Lorraine Raguseo have all taught me valuable things. Bob Rone, Paul Sandler, Don Stecher, George Ushkowitz, Lisa Weildlich, Barbara Powell, Lena Brattsten, Paul Chan, Michelle Keats, Dennis DiFlorio, Adrienne Soresi, Paula Cella, Fr. Steve Curry O.S.A. and Ed Blake have all shared special wines.

Steve, Frank and Ron Dandrea, Bill and Deanna Higgins, June Kim, Erin Mahoney, and Sean Mahoney, have shared their enthusiasm toward wine and taught me to notice more.

I continue to learn from newer Dionysians like Jack Tomasello, Adrienne Turner, Robert Rone, Sharon Byrne, and Carolyn Nemia.

Paul Wagner, John Hames of the AWS, "Pooch" Pucilowski of the SWE, Steve Hendricks, Andy Fruzzetti, Chef Michael Huber and Jack Morey who rode with me from Aswan to Cairo discussing and drinking wine all night, I thank you for sharing both wine and knowledge, and to all I've missed here but have not forgotten. Thank you.

Introduction

I had an idea to write some short stories that would be of special interest to wine-lovers.

I know there are dozens of books available that teach you how wine is made, the grapes used for wine making and the best areas in which good wine grapes are grown. There are books that have lists of the best old wines and the best wines presently available. There are books that stress how to better enjoy wine by training your senses and there are books for wine lovers who want to know about barrels, corkscrews and bottles. Then, I realized, as John Steinbeck said, "Ideas are like rabbits. You get a couple and learn how to handle them, and pretty soon you have a dozen." I wanted each of my stories to have a specific wine or, at least *wine* in general, as its base for an ironic twist, or a focal point or even just a subtle insert that makes the tale have a deeper verisimilitude for the wine-lover.

I wanted to provide a book for people who already know a lot about wine as well as a book for a novice who just finds wine and its culture interesting. I wanted a book you can read while in bed just one part at a time, a book with enough wine talk in it to permit you to give as a gift to a wine-drinking friend or to someone who loves literature. I wanted a little book that can be re-read from time to time to recall a pleasant reference about a wine or, while re-reading, note something new.

The ideas kept expanding but were confusing. It was

Charles Dickens who stated that an idea, like a ghost... must be spoken to a little before it will explain itself and so I tried to coax the plot developments from the ghostly ideas that made appearances in empty old wine bottles. While working on this idea, and still in the conversation phase, I read a remark made by Thornton Wilder that he called his defense: "I do borrow from other writers, shamelessly! I can only say in my defense, like the woman brought before a judge on the charges of kleptomania, 'I do steal, but, your Honor, only from the very best of stores.'"

So I reread as much of O. Henry as I could during the summer a few years ago and then wrote, "The Blind Taster". I started to reread other writers I've loved for years. I counted each author's use of three-syllable words, dashes, internal questions, and recorded the average sentence length and so on until I could give a classroom lecture on the fundamental style techniques of the writer I was presently absorbing. I had decided to write about people whose lives, like mine, had been changed, maybe not always for the best as I show in "Wine Labels", where I really tried to capture Charlotte Gilman's Poe-like technique, or, about lives who became more enjoyable and even more meaningful by learning about and savoring wines from everywhere and I wanted to create each story in a different writer's best known style. Oh, that's all you say. Yes, I answer and that's why I've been on this project for the past nine years.

I wanted the reader, whom I had to assume already owned many wine encyclopedias, introduction to wine books, wine-making text and lots of books about wine regions, grapes and maybe just a few on how to smell and taste, to simply enjoy reading a short story and then find it more intriguing, and more fascinating than those people who did not know the slightest bit about wine. I hoped my readers would like to find something they could read in bed or on the beach, you know, easy reading, not academic studies, that might be entertaining and have an extra delightful enhancement of pleasure added to this reading because they would know the wines mentioned either from reading about them or having tasted them. In some cases, the wine itself might even play the role of a character; in others, a very minor part but still a bit of interest to a wine-lover. If a wine or a grape is mentioned that they didn't know about, well then, all the better because wine-lovers always want to know more about the topic they love and they'll be glad they read the story.

My thirty-five years of teaching about wine and writing wine education articles for magazines and radio Weekend Wine Tip spots and even short TV wine clips provided the enology data. My forty-five years of teaching literature at both the high school and college level helped with the style research. Why then has it taken so long? Well, I learned that you think and even talk a bit like the writer you've been studying or even sound and think like the people you've been conversing with most recently. To change that means you have to rearrange your thinking and then practice by doing writings to be discarded before you can change your literary attitude. It took an entire winter to reread all the Zane Gray books my father left me to capture Gray's tone and style, if I ever did, before writing "The Hunting Camp". I wanted enthusiasm for both the thrill of hunting and the love of wine to marry in as short a story as I could get. I didn't want the usual Zane Gray Western story; I wanted

Zane Gray's voice telling an Eastern outdoor tale. I always aimed for short short stories. I believe that every long short story I've ever read could have been shortened.

The short story is a specific genre and has certain limitations; length is not a requirement. I eschew long short stories.

In 1918, *The Elements of Style,* by William Strunk, Jr. became the first and maybe the best book on writing style. "Omit needless words," Strunk insisted and he also wrote, "A sentence should contain no unnecessary words, a paragraph no unnecessary sentences." It is the writing basis that Ernest Hemmingway best exhibited. Well, trying to write a Hemmingway story took me just two days to complete and then, about two months to edit over and over again. I found I could open any of his works to any page in the text and just start reading and after a day or two of this, I could put words down on paper like he did, not with his genius for specifics, but with a similar tone. However, even now I'll never know if they were the right words. We all know that "brevity is the soul of wit," and that it goes back to Shakespeare with Polonius's advice in *Hamlet,* but you can be certain this teaching concept goes back even further, maybe all the way back to *Ecclesiastics* where it states, "there's nothing new under the sun." So readers of wine stories would not expect you to ramble on and on and the plots can be as old as mankind. It's what you do with them that counts.

With some writers, I found I could capture the tone but not the complete style. F. Scott Fitzgerald was difficult and, of course, James Joyce. In "The Wake", I wanted the reader, as well as one character, to experience an epiphany about wine. With others, it seems that there's an invisible underlining literary music that my ear could note, but my thinking could not completely reproduce. In these efforts, I hope the wines mentioned, because of their fame or interest, overshadows the weaker writing style. The literature-loving wine drinker will be my toughest critic. In any case, I have tried to provide some tales that can be read over and over again, especially after a delightful evening of fine food, good friends and some great wine.

Biblical style is basic but hard to recreate as I learned when I attempted, "The Wedding Feast". O. Henry's vocabulary was amazing and Somerset Maugham, maybe one of the best short story writers ever, had a sentence variation that I had never noticed as a student or as a teacher using his works in class. Richard Burton may be the best Arabic translator ever and he captured, as I tried to emulate, the powerful use of similes and metaphors that dominate Middle Eastern thinking. His *Arabian Nights* is sublime. My, "The Wedding Feast", relies entirely on the reader's previous knowledge for a literary appreciation of the story or simply a good knowledge of Syrah (and all its names) to be intriguing for the less wine-knowledgeable reader.

Edmund Burke wrote, "to read without reflecting is like eating without digesting," and I hope these stories, on first reading will provide some entertainment and with further contemplation, provide some subtle wit not first noticed. These stories are like your children; you love them all the same even if one is more successful than the others. "The French Café", took a very long time to finish, not to write, but to edit. Over and over again, I made changes and then re-read Hemmingway to get my mind into a mode of thinking with words and sentences that, at least, sounded like the master of brevity and with the same clarity. I may be the happiest with this attempt.

Mark Twain used a number of different dialects and each is polished throughout his works. Trying to reproduce this style may have taken me longer to do than it took Clemens to write entire novels. When you want a drunken boy to change his dialect from just uneducated to slave-influenced uneducated Southern sounds with the influence of alcohol added to it, you fear your product may be misunderstood. He was the master, I merely an apprentice.

Where are the Byron, Shelley or Keats examples? Well, like Frost and Longfellow, this work excludes their genre. I considered Sir Walter Scott and Thomas Hardy but decided there was too little difference and too much a distance since their works were in the common household. Time and space prevent Joyce Carol Oates, D. H. Lawrence and William Faulkner from being included. John Updike was a good possibility, but his Rabbit character drank beer. J.R.R. Tolkein tends to need far more space than a short story usually allocates but I would hope to try it sometime anyway.

A standard wine book can be divided many different ways but in the end, they all talk about where what type of grapes are grown and how the wines are made and what food they best complement. It's all necessary and helpful to better enjoy wine. A short story, on the other had, can also be divided many ways, but in the end, it has limited key characters, a fundamental plot, maybe an ironic twist, stream of conscious thinking or lots of action with little meditation or is filled with only thought provoking ideas and lots of details about the setting and no action at all. Writers decide which to use. Each great writer uses just the right amount of words; no more, no less, and creates a successful story by making it enjoyable to read and even re-read. When you find something of interest in a story you are reading, something you know about or have experienced, like some historic site you've visited, a painting you've seen or a bottle of wine you have tasted or, at least, a hopeful wish that you might someday taste it, it makes the story complement your intelligence and awareness and you're so much the better for it.

There are short, short stories and long short stories. I've tried my best to produce, as best I can, in most cases, shorter short stories. However, to be true to each writer's fundamental style, I had to recreate not only sentence length, vocabulary similarities, character's names or a play on the name and also the tone with local color and point of view, and most importantly, I've had to write what I believe may be an honest estimate of each writers' average story length.

Gilman, who wrote some stories with insights into the mind, proved to be very difficult to imitate in both structure and in plot. She was very advanced in her thinking for the early 20th Century and her attempt to convey the horror of madness inspired my attempt. I've always believed wine, as a symbol of civilization, can prevent madness, but I suppose it can marry and live with madness too. You decide.

Trying to be discreetly simple, both wine and literature can sometimes mislead or confuse both the taster and the reader.

All the stories are printed in the order in which they were

written over the years with one exception. "The Tell-Tale Thought", my humble attempt at Edgar Alan Poe's theme and style, was written last but inserted earlier to balance the total number of wine references throughout the stories and also because Poe was the first author of whom I'd ever read his complete works – everything he ever wrote. Even with that task completed, I still had to return to over a dozen of his stories before attempting to imitate him.

Whether reading these pages is like savoring a fifty-year-old Château d'Yquem or quaffing basic Beaujolais, I'm sure you'll remember both the complexity and simplicity of true enjoyment when you are better aware of all the subtle details. I hope stumbling onto a wine you've had or heard of will make all the difference. –JJM

Every Bottle Has a Story

A Tell-Tale Thought

With the utmost respect for Edgar Allen Poe

I would neither expect nor attempt to demand belief regarding the narrative that I now relate. Yes! I am nervous – dreadfully nervous about my situation. I am neither paranoid nor mad – I simply know that to-morrow or the next day, he will murder me.

My thoughts have detailed the event. I see it constantly.

I sit and savor an Amalthea Cellars 2007 Europa VII, lush with cabernet sauvignon, merlot and cabernet franc. I had just finished another New Jersey wine, a Tomasello Cabernet Sauvignon Reserve and waited to be wronged. I know he felt slighted when last I served my final 1998 Romanée St. Vivant and an Echezeaux to one of his friends. You may fancy this act as an insane deed – my guest thought not. He, however, related the experience to what has now become a cunning stalker – a man who believed he missed the vinous experience of scoring a DRC La Tache and a Richebourg. He had gotten serious misinformation about which wines were actually poured – his jealousy festered into a hatred toward me and I become stressed at even the mention of pinot noir. I drank wines from New Mexico and New York last week, a plethora of wine, but fear continues to manifest itself whenever I dine.

You may ask if it's the caprices of all madmen to anticipate pandemonium – to lie sleepless in a somber of gloom – but I am certain of his impetuous fury toward me.

I think constantly of every possible scenario.

We once sat together comparing a pinot gris from Oregon and a syrah from the Cape May Winery's Isaac Smith Estate which has the coffin-shaped label, aptly named after an undertaker from the Victorian Village of Olde Cape May. After I told him how improbable any statement of truth could be made unless we compared, at least, the same grape, if not the same vintage, his eyes showed faintly luminous notes of fire and the fury of the demon that possessed him told me in no uncertain terms that I would pay for my sagacious expedient of not trying to cancel the fact that he had been slighted! I instantly knew that he would murder me. He would not be satisfied with my demise alone – no, it would have to be painful and slow.

I could not but wonder why he spent so much time with me at all. I had nothing to do with his loss of employment. Yes – I was the one promoted but I never knew until the day I arrived to take my new position at Wells_____ that I'd been given his seat – his position of power in the company – his very *raison d'être!*

From my first week at the establishment, he'd taken a liking to me. I now comprehend that it was all part of his sinister plan to eradicate me in some hideous manner – someway to sedate his lust for blood. When I first avoided him during the company's biweekly wine tastings, he would tell me to not be so paranoid. As I am now sick with worry about my well-being, I laugh at the irony of his initial attack upon me. I gave his comments little thought at the time. Later on, we did sit at the same judging table when asked to represent the firm at regional wine competitions where we endeavored to identify the grape, the area of production, sometimes the vintage and, if possible, the vintner or winery from which a half dozen or so samples where poured. I felt I had answered correctly more often than he – but neither of us kept a count. Each time I had my guess rewarded with affirmative statements from the event director, I noticed his stare of malice. I sensed a cataleptic disorder in his countenance but I had to channel my apprehensions due to the fact that he was indeed of a higher ranking than I within the company. It was not until I had received the advancement of which I earlier spoke, that I thought I could relax in his company. We would be equal partners – at work and in our love of wine. Never in the entire world of probability did I anticipate the unfathomable odds of my promotion being the cause of his extinction within the company! He was fired to make room for me.

It was a mere month before his dismissal, that he invited me to view and help arrange his corkscrew collection. It was, I'm obliged to honestly report, nearly as large and as unique as the famous Brother Timothy's of the _____Winery who, in California, kept his collection of corkscrews – a collection that became world renown featuring every type of ingenious invention for opening the delight of Bacchus and permitting the gift of Dionysus to flow freely. With so valuable a collection of corkscrews and a cellar worth a fortune, I had to wonder why he now worked at all – he must have been independently wealthy, and why he would befriend such a humble associate as me?

Fear – anxiety – tension? Yes and more. I knew he watched me. I felt with every breath that he would soon take his revenge. I had to make amends. On the usual weekend of my scheduled wine tasting, I canceled with everyone and invited him to join me to review a few different wines. I meticulously poured a Horton Vineyard Viognier, which I had obtained during the previous summer's drive into Virginia along Route 33 to pay my respects at an old friend's viewing. I learned the wine had eleven percent manseng added and thus, I knew where the hints of pineapple and coconut came from. He never noticed it. I poured another viognier, concocted in a similar style from the Bellview Winery located in the Outer Coastal Plain but he could not tell the difference. On my last visit to Baltimore to attend a funeral, I obtained a Boordy Vineyard red and he thought it European. I offered little conversation and kept pouring wines; the pinot noir from Michigan's Dizzy Daisy Winery located just outside Bay Axe was thin — he assumed it was a New York wine. He did enjoy, however, the other Michigan wine, the Forty-Five North Vineyard and Winery's white. I was beginning to see a less dangerous foe but still I sensed his potential to hasten upon me a demon's fury. If it was not my sharing with him wines that no one else could show, it must still be the company's decision to promote me that ate at his soul! I calmed myself with a Sharrott Chardonnay.

I felt a most notorious ill-fortune settle on me like the curtain of night descending on my soul. Try as I did, I could not lift the ominous feelings I carried within me day and night. He sensed my tension and again told me to get help in eradicating my paranoid feelings. When he asked me what I feared so greatly, I lied. I told him I could not relinquish my childhood nightmares. I knew he knew I feared him, but I would never let him be certain of that fact. Terror was what I felt during every dark hour. But I could not leave because of my new position and I could not avoid him because I lived by the motto: *amicos prope tenete propius inimicos*, "keep your friends close, and your enemies closer." He never mentioned his previous job or how he lost it nor did he ever talk about the rare Burgundies he thought he had missed because I had neglected to invite him. His congeniality was obviously a façade. I did, however, during our most recent weekend tasting, learn that he truly loved and understood the quest of seeking a great wine. I once poured a 1997 Vietti Barolo Castiglione and he recognized its depth and elegance. He also expounded great prose regarding the Niholaihof Grüner Veltliner Hafeahzug I served blind. He loved its peppery spice.

After this unique tasting – he invited me back to his home saying that he had added some new utensils to his collection. I went. I finally began to feel less stress – I relaxed a bit. We road silently to his home. I knew I could not stay late, maybe review the new items, taste a bottle he most assuredly would open and then return with enough time to review the company reports I had to evaluate by the morning meeting. Upon arriving, he went directly to the wine cellar and asked if there was any bottle I'd care to taste? I instantly responded by pointing to a 1976 Savigny Les Beaune that was lying very near to a 2002 Pernand Vergelesses. He silently responded by lifting the old Burgundy and started cutting its foil. He withdrew the cork ever so slowly and poured an ounce for me to assess. I swirled, sniffed and savored a droplet on the tip of my tongue. I could not resist the smile and nodded approval. He then poured two glasses and suggested we go see the newest corkscrews. I, for the first time in months, was relaxed.

He offered me a seat and as I sat savoring the nectar of the gods, he withdrew a drawer from the table. It was filled with both ancient and modern corkscrews. I lifted a modern one to study the helix closely while he expounded upon the oldest item he now owned. It came, he lectured, from the time of the Spanish Inquisition and was used for more things than one could imagine. The wine was so silky and smooth that I drank quickly – too quickly. He refilled my glass and I thought to myself that I should have not drunk so much earlier in the day – it prevented me from a perfect appreciation of the wine I was now reviewing. He exhibited what at first seemed to be a beguiling smile but as reality proved – it quickly turned into a sinister sneer as he again added more Burgundy to my glass.

It was then that I realized he was standing uncomfortably close behind me still holding his Spanish corkscrew. I started to rise, but he put his hand on my shoulder from behind and drove the Inquisition devise deep into my neck rupturing my jugular vein. I could see the wine-red blood spurt into the air above my ear as inconceivable terror took hold of my mind, my heart and my soul! I heard him laughingly shout that it is *not* paranoia if it *is* real and I should have shared my La Tache! My last thought was I had been correct all along.

The Blind Taster

Apologies to O. Henry

Everyone had arrived ahead of him. Both host and guests had been briefed on his ability to identify wines from only their smell and taste. It was very cool for such a late spring evening in 2003, a year that become one of the hottest on record in New York's lower Manhattan as well as in Europe. The people at the party expected a wine celebrity, a man to teach and entertain them and nearly all were hoping to acquire some secret data or procedure for guessing what was in a wine bottle without seeing the label.

As the special guest and his wife meandered up the front steps, they could hear party laughter and it made them both pleased and appreciative for having been invited to a party where they might only know one or two people. The wife, an educated lady working as a public school teacher, was exceptionally well read. She enjoyed going to wine parties, special dinners and even major trade tastings but made no special effort to delve into the mysterious nature of wine. All her friends relied on her opinion when they went out to lunch or got together for dinner after a Broadway Show. Because her husband both taught about wine and wrote about wine, it was assumed that she too would find it easy to pair the proper wine with the proper entrée. She always complied with the wishes of her friends and selected a wine and she enjoyed and continued sharing unique wine experiences with her friends after she attended some special event or show. She was not as gregarious as her husband, but she knew she would be able to mingle and procure at least one good story for her faculty lounge the following Monday.

The husband, a dedicated wine lover who had studied intensely about wine, its history, its production and about all the proper serving and cultural necessities, and, more recently, reviewed all the publications seeking newly researched health benefits derived from wine, knew he would be asked dozens of questions on every facet of the wine world. He had, over the years, become the man you contacted if you wanted to know anything about wine or about a civilized life style. He established this reputation because he was usually very helpful as well as accurate. He would also explain to his inquisitors that if he did not know an answer, he would not lie; they could count on him researching the question and getting an answer back to them as soon as possible.

They approached the house with winter still lingering in the spring air and after only one knock on the front door, it opened. The host, Anthony Dacasa, in a loud clear voice, announced to everyone already in the room that his favorite wine tasting partner had arrived. He had two wine glasses sitting on a small Port table next to the door and without first offering to take either of the couple's jackets, he poured two small samples into the glasses from a bottle buried in a brown paper bag.

"What is it?" he asked. Both the man and his wife began to swirl the water-colored liquid in their glasses. The wife quickly sipped her wine and looked at her husband. He continued to swirl and smell. Swirl and smell. Smell and swirl.

"It's a Riesling, a German Riesling. I think it's a 2001, but let me think," as he paused for a few seconds. "The Riesling was grown in the Mosel-Saar-Ruwer and fermented in a stainless steel tank." He sniffed again, "yes, all steel, no wood. And, I still do believe that it is the 2001."

He then, slowly brought the glass of wine to his lips and savored a small taste. He nodded his head and turned to receive his wife's approval. She offered no reaction at all. The host of the party, turned toward the guests whom he had been entertaining, and filled with pride for having invited his best and most knowledgeable wine drinking friend, explained that it was indeed a German Riesling from the 2001 vintage and even better, it came from the German wine growing area called the Mosel-Saar-Ruwer.

Some people applauded, others smiled with positive support in their eyes. Helen, a long-time friend of the host, immediately walked up to him and shook his hand.

The remainder of the party waned in enthusiasm after the spectacular presentation at the door. Instead of hanging onto the host and inquiring what other interesting friends he had, they dismissed mature respectability and acted like childish rock-star groupies. The host rapidly felt he might have made a mistake. Maybe he should have simply hosted a wine and cheese gathering and he could have led any discussions on the wines or cheese. Maybe he and his wine-loving friend could have done a presentation together? He was certain that he had lost status and decided that he too could garner the center of attention by correctly identifying a wine at a blind tasting, a wine served directly and only to him, and the wine to be poured would be hidden in a similar brown paper bag to create the mystery of it all.

He checked his busy calendar and realized that he didn't need to host another party. All of his friends who attended this party, the professional wine lover and a good number of the other people at his house that evening would be attending a charity fundraiser at the area's top restaurant. Helen Delphia both owned the restaurant and was chairperson for the fundraiser. Helen was a very close friend who knew many California wine makers and people in the wine trade. It would be a perfect time for him to catch the spotlight.

What this want-to-be wine connoisseur never heard was the conversation the featured guest and his wife had when they got home after the party where he had correctly guessed and identified the mystery German wine.

As they entered their home, she asked him if he really knew really what the wine was or did he just make a lucky guess?

"Riesling is easy," he answered her. "I could smell that. You and everyone else who have ever had a Riesling could tell that. But if you noticed the bag, it almost, but not completely, covered a tall green bottle, a German wine bottle shape, and the green glass tells us that it is from the Mosel area of Germany. Brown glass would have been from the Rhine areas. The rings around the top of the capsule could have told me what the classification was, an *Auslese*, *Spätlese* or *Kabinett*. Even a *Beeren'* or a *Trockenbeerenauslese* but I didn't want to go that far. I saw it was an Auslese wine. All of the highest German wine categories are labeled. They come from the *Qualitätswein mit Prädikat* selections; quality wines with special attributes."

"Well, you could have at least tasted it first! I know you wanted to help Anthony impress his friends but you did it too quickly," she answered with an air of contempt. He then realized why she was so neutral in her reaction to his friend's guessing game.

Later that month they were preparing to attend the charity wine party at their favorite restaurant where Anthony had planned to correctly describe a wine in a blind tasting. No one knew that the dedicated connoisseur was taking a guest who worked for the wine industry and no one knew that Anthony had volunteered to help Helen Delphia set up the food selections and the wines for the party. Anthony was able to see the first wine that would be served and he carefully studied the description on the reverse side of the bottle. Then, he stayed outside the restaurant to greet some early arriving guests permitting them to enter, complete their obeisance and begin tasting the evening's first wine.

Anthony's dedicated wine lovers arrived right on time and they entered together. As they walked in, Mr. Dacasa was introduced to the Director of Wine for National Promotions. She worked on the East Coast for a promotional wine consulting company every now and then, and was always happy to meet her friend's other wine companions.

As soon as the four entered the fund-raising event and even before anyone offered to take their coats, a server approached Anthony with a glass and a brown paper bag. An ideal correct tasting sample of about two ounces of red wine was poured from the concealed bottle and as Anthony began to swirl the wine and sniff at it, the server, who almost said out loud, "Uncle Ant…" coughed and corrected himself and then asked, "I've been told to ask you what the wine is, sir?"

As he swirled and sniffed, sniffed and sipped, the would-be-connoisseur drifted into the crowd to be among the guests. Finally, he was ready to announce his decision.

Anthony said, "It's a California Gamay. It has a slight banana aroma and hints of fruity strawberry. It has to be a 2002. I can tell it was fermented in temperature controlled stainless steal and finished in older French oak to round it out."

The young waiter pulled the bottle out of the paper bag and announced that the wine was a California Gamay from 2002. Applause followed and as Anthony shook hands, he sought out Helen Delphia and his friends to garner their reaction to his vinous victory. But as he approached from their backs, he heard Helen saying she too knew that wine. The three people listening to her were the Chairpersons of the fund-raising committee and none were friends of nor knew Mr. Dacasa. She told them that she had been hired to write the description for the back label of the wine used in the blind tasting, not from taste but from traditional Beaujolais descriptors and said that Anthony had it memorized exactly. The only problem was that the wine should not have been labeled as Gamay; it didn't have the necessary seventy-five percent to be called that. It was mostly Merlot with some Gamay added. The company had already corrected the mistake.

Anthony immediately sprinted toward another dining room and planned to leave as early as possible hoping he would never be asked to repeat a demonstration of his wine tasting abilities.

Worth the Wait

With respect to Somerset Maugham

Every wine lover anxiously waits for that special moment, anniversary or birthday to open and share his or her best cellar selection. When the time comes, the problem arises as to where you will pair your special bottle with special food and with whom will you share it?

Where do you open and properly serve Champagne like the 1976 Salon from Magnums, 1975 Heitz Cabernet Sauvignon from the Martha's Vineyard, 1945 Chateau Lafite Rothschild or a 1961 Chateau d'Yquem?

People who have come to understand that wine is the liquid part of every meal because it makes all foods taste their best, can either cook themselves and properly open, decant and serve their vinous treasures along with the perfect match, or they can visit their favorite restaurant with permission to take along their own wines and hope to find entrées that will highlight wines that have been cellared for years or even decades. The opportunity to *bring your own bottle* with you to a restaurant for dinner makes states like New Jersey a wine-lover's paradise. In other states, even the opportunity to pay a corkage fee to have the restaurant staff open and serve your own wine bottles makes it easier to enjoy well-aged and rare wine selections.

Going out to dine properly means visiting a place that truly knows wine and food. They have to provide large clear glassware. They need white tablecloths and proper lighting so your eyes can tease your tongue as they absorb the colors and begin predicting what will come!

You need Champagne flutes so clean that the wine will bubble for hours, carafes to decant great wines and an enthusiasm in the staff to please.

I am fortunate. I know a place that has it all. I am also fortunate to have friends who wanted to share my sixtieth birthday and also share some of their special wines with me. They called one of my top three BYOB restaurants still in business at the time, *Toujours* in Marlton, New Jersey way south of New York on the eastern seaboard of the United States and just east of Philadelphia. Of course, it's less known than many New York or San Francisco restaurants, and we were willing to travel anywhere to celebrate the event. Paris, Rome or Hong Kong was not out of the question. Chef Jennifer, a charming youthful Vietnamese culinary genius, worked with Dr. Michaels of New Brunswick to create a menu that would highlight the wines we were saving for a very special occasion.

Dr. Garylis, who had to fly back from Ohio and landed in a Philadelphia snowstorm to make the dinner, began the project a month earlier, when it was first suggested that my wine friends celebrate my entrance into a new decade of life, by saying, "It's time we opened the best wine we presently have in our cellars!"

Dr. Vincent added that his wife Sue, a Dionysian member as well as an artist, would create menus to record the *Event du Cuisine* of the decade! Even though I had told my wife repeatedly that I did not want a party, she encouraged the event. And if, at my expense, it was a surprise party, I told her I would embarrass the entire group by simply leaving. She, and my wine-loving friends went ahead anyway and planned a meal to remember but did not make it a surprise event. I many times have to thank my wife for doing things I don't want to do.

Heavy snow was predicted for the January night of the event. Considerations were made about canceling, but everyone agreed that it would work out because the great Dionysus would protect his followers. When we arrived at *Toujours*, we were extremely flattered by being the only guests to be served that evening. The owner was our personal waiter and his wife, the master chef, came to the table between each course to ascertain our opinions. Because of the snow, which was already falling, and the predicted heavy amounts, the owners had sent all their staff home early and closed the restaurant for the night, closed, that is, for all except we dedicated Dionysians.

"Did the food marry with the wines? Was the presentation pleasing to your eyes? Did the flavors highlight the wine? Was everything the correct temperature?" you ask me.

"Yes, it was high cuisine at its paramount perfection!"

Arriving at six afforded time to savor the 1990 Laurent-Perriere Cuvee Rosé Brut before drinking what many consider the greatest Champagne of the 20th century, the 1976 Salon "Le Mesnil" served from Magnum. Mesnil is the vineyard that Krug features in its best of all Champagne. The Champagne married with San Francisco Golden Pouches, Spring Rolls and Salmon Dumplings.

Course number two was Butternut Squash with Diver's Scallop Caviar tasted with the 1998 Olivier Lefaive

Chassagne-Montrachet, a bottle carried back from the winery by Dr. Garylis. It led to interesting anecdotes about travel and wine tastings in distant lands. Great wine matched to great food is always the best catalyst for great conversation.

A course that was totally hedonistic was the Foie Gras with Pineapple Chutney. It was savored with a 2002 Domaine Cailbourdin "Les Cris" Pouilly Fumé. Chef Jennifer said that she wanted to make the Foie Gras differently for this special wine-filled birthday. It actually kissed your tongue. It was the finest example I've ever tasted any where in the world. The pineapple brought out subdued flavors hidden deep in the Pouilly Fumé.

They toasted to my birthday; I toasted to friends who organized the dinner and toasted to the chef and host who made the event formal. Equal interest in civilization as well as wine, was reflected through the appreciation of wine and food and it made the event spiritual. Teasing and joking about my love affair with great wines made the dinner humbling.

Snow continued to fall outside, but the warm gaiety inside made us eschew any concern about the drive home.

The two entrées followed: fresh rock fish, unique and difficult to find, with a Cognac Reduction over Lobster Ravioli and the red Burgundy, the 1999 Domaine Confuron-Cotetidot Vosne-Romaneé, from the single vineyard, "Les Suchots", brought out flavors that were unimaginable. Both the fish and the wine politely introduced a Stuffed Filet Mignon with Apple Merlot Reduction, which was highlighted with the 1975 Heitz "Martha's Vineyard" Cabernet Sauvignon. It was the major entrée and it was fit for a king. I was humbled to have friends share it with me.

Wines that had been properly aged, still showing bright colors and no signs of fading along with foods in colorful artistic designs on white china remind you of slowly walking through the world's greatest art museums. Great friends, great conversation and great food created for epicureans on Mt. Olympus was completed, naturally, with a cheese course of Roquefort, Papilan, Livarot and Cherot served with a 1945 Chateau Lafite Rothschild. Considered the greatest wine of the entire 20th Century, and the perfectly matched cheeses made it a combination to linger over. It was one of the truly great treasures in my wine cellar and I had the perfect people with which to share it. It was time for me to make a toast. I wondered what the really rich people of the world were doing that night? I couldn't imagine anyone dining or drinking better than we humble servants of Dionysus.

"*In vino veritas*," I toasted. "Indeed, in wine there is truth. You've shared your best wines with me tonight but I toast to all who seek a better life, deeper understanding of what is beautiful and to everyone who shared their knowledge of civilization with us so that we might come together on this snowy January evening to appreciate being alive!" There were no comments. Everyone smiled and was aware of how far we'd come from our hard-working immigrant families to educated productive members of a modern civilization. We lived many types of different lives. Wine had brought us all together.

Fearing the bottle of Lafite might have been too old, even though it came from the century's finest Bordeaux year, I was reluctant to decant it before going to the restaurant.

Too much air for old wines can cause them to fade too early. Too little air for big wines prevents them from opening up and exhibiting all their charm. I knew the traveling might shake it up too much so I prepared it before the hour's drive to the restaurant. My wife held it upright while we drove. She leaned it to the right when we curved left and to the left when we curved right. I was lucky. It decanted easily. It was perfect.

A dessert married to the 1961 Chateau D'Yquem, the greatest of all Sauternes, had to be the highest quality crème brûlée. It was silky smooth and rich. You could not tell where one flavor ended and the other began. Sauternes to brûlée or brûlée to Sauternes. It didn't matter. The golden amber liquid danced in your mouth with the custard. The wine and dessert were like a long-time husband and wife.

Looking back on that moment, I now realize that everyone should have kissed. We all miss too many romantic moments in our lives. Time waits for no one. Savor the moment and never pass on savoring the aroma before sipping the wine.

To conclude the evening, during which I was given a bag with 60 birthday gifts for my sixtieth birthday, we sampled the 1944 Armagnac from Sempe, a brandy that was bottled on November 16 in 1987 after resting in barrels for 43 years. Miss Dans, who prepared the gift bag, never stopped savoring the Armagnac's aroma. It enriched the final coffee of the evening without being added to it. It was velvety smooth and it was (born) harvested the same year as I was. An old bottle of wine, Armagnac or Champagne, Bordeaux or Barolo, is a time machine for a journey into the past. It's captured sunshine from the year you were born.

It was worth the wait. *Toujours,* a French-Vietnamese Restaurant of the highest cuisine, understood not only food, but the owners also knew that dedicated wine lovers understand that the sum effect is always greater than the individual parts of a meal.

Great wine and food should be a necessity of life, not a luxury and the love and respect of dear friends should be something we all work to gain by sharing our energy, our knowledge and, of course, our very best wines.

We all drove home safely with each couple in their own car quietly contemplating the unique event they'd just experienced. There was no one else on the road. The snow engulfed a moment in time and reshaped our lives as it reshaped the structures and landscape around us.

Just before leaving, my final toast to my hosts and friends that night was, "May we all live forever...or die trying."

A Chef Second to None

For F. Scott Fitzgerald

I was younger and much more vulnerable when I received the phone call requesting me to attend a private dinner party, a dining experience that might well be the envy of international gourmets; I accepted immediately. I didn't bother to ask about the menu nor the wines, which I knew would companion each course. My host, a doctor of viticulture, had won a charity raffle. His prize was having renowned chef, Anthony d'Larnio, create, prepare and serve a private dinner party for up to fourteen very special guests.

Dr. Andrews would be providing some wines from his personal cellar and we were asked to each bring a wine to match a course designed and created by the esteemed chef. Chef d'Larnio, who had done numerous interviews for magazine articles, and television, had been portrayed as a great connoisseur of fine wines as well as being one of the world's best chefs. He had been photographed in of many of the world's best restaurant's wine cellars. He always insisted on one and only one wine to pair with each of his masterful food creations. "No! No!" he once screamed on an early morning television interview. "Only Barolo will work with this wild boar. And, it must be at least fifteen years old."

My excitement grew with each passing day as I learned more and more about the upcoming event. Dr. Andrews called repeatedly to not only entice, but to inquire about other guests' plans to bring a wide array of the world's finest bottles. He always began each phone call with comments about how much he respected my palate and my ability to pair wine with even the world's most unique foods.

"I can only make suggestions," I replied.

"Suggestions? Please, do you think Chef d'Larnio's wild mushroom bisque will work better with my Barbera or with the Ridge Zinfandel that Michael wants to bring?"

"Zin can enhance mushroom flavors, clean the palate and create a desire for even more culinary gratification," I answered. "But if the bisque is on the more delicate side, the Barbera's light cherry and subtle earthiness would be perfect." The good doctor grew more impatient with each phone call. He never realized that I viewed these chances to dine with interesting wine people and a superior chef as a post-doctorial learning symposium. As the date drew nearer, I began to review our honored chef's newest cookbook and I called a New York friend, who once had dinner with Mr. d'Larnio, to ask about his personality, his demeanor and his ability to share his knowledge. Sadly, I was told that Chef d'Larnio, according to just this one friend, tended to avoid questions, detailed questions, about his preparations and his own wine collection. I did learn that it was not the Italian wines he claimed to love the best. Instead, he once openly stated at a select James Beard charity dinner function, which was held in a private brownstone in the Upper East Side, that Bordeaux was his passion. "I know more about Bordeaux than any living chef," he explained during the cheese course.

Armed with this small bit of knowledge about our

esteemed visitor, I decided to offer Dr. Andrews one of my finest old bottles and promised to stand it up two days before we opened it to prepare it for a proper decanting. I agreed to decant it myself at the start of the meal and permit the vinous treasure time to breath and fully open up by the time the cheese course was presented. My host also requested that I use a traditional candle to look for the sediment instead of my usual four-inch flashlight. After all, he told me, one of his British friends might be able to join us if he could get to the states in time and using a torch, as Robert the Englishman would have called it, would just be uncouth. He had a proper carafe available, so all I needed to do was carefully carry the feature wine without shaking and disturbing the sediments. I agreed to work by candlelight even though the banquet was not to be black tie; Dr. Andrews had used the term "smart casual" on his printed invitation, which we all received just one week prior to the dinner. He was certain that a man who said he had cooked for the rich and the famous, European monarchs and for some Academy Award winners, would be impressed with the 1949 Chateau Pichon-Longueville-Comtesse de Lalande. He grinned every time he repeated the wine I had offered for him to share with his dinner guests.

The Saturday evening event was approaching quickly and while I was boasting about being able to experience foods and wines that I was certain would be written about in local newspapers as well as national magazines, I met a man from Philadelphia at an Atlantic City casino who, after sharing some basic local conversation, told me, after I brought up the nearing food and wine gala, that he had once dined with Chef d'Larnio and he told me to expect a pompous egomaniac. I was a bit rattled.

"Oh, it was about four years ago, right after d'Larnio opened his Washington D.C. spot. He had been on "Good Morning America" where all he did was boast about his many restaurants quickly becoming three star dining centers. He proudly explained how he had corrected the TV host regarding the fact that Gavi was not a grape but a place in northern Italy.

"Well," I slowly interjected, "a lot of people make that mistake but why did he make such a big deal about it?" Cortese was the grape that made Gavi, but really, who cares?

"He wants everyone to think that he knows it all. Everything. More than anyone."

"He gets more coverage than anyone I know," I stated. "Remember when Robert Parker seemed to control the wine world? Remember when new wine lovers would not buy a bottle unless the *Wine Spectator* rated it at least a ninety? Now, it's d'Larnio who sets the Standards."

We talked a bit further, but I could tell I had failed to impress him with my good luck in being asked to share in a major culinary and wine moment.

Saturday evening was perfect. The weather had cleared and all day the sky was Mediterranean blue. My bottle of Pichon was ready. I was hungry, which as Ben Franklin said, is the best sauce. Well, he really said, "hunger is the best pickle," but few people today remember when pickle relish was served as an appetizer.

Upon arriving, we were introduced to Chef d'Larnio who explained that he was certain we would all be impressed. La Grand Dame was served in tall clear flutes. Course after course married well with the wines each guest had brought. The waiters carried our accolades back to the chef in the kitchen where, I'm certain, he glowed with pride. The cheeses, all three, the blue Cabrales, the aged Manchego and the old English Cheddar were at proper room temperature. I lit the candle provided me by Dr. Andrews and preceded to decant the '49 Pichon slowly and with all the pomp and circumstance that a historic wine should be afforded. Chef d'Larnio's major work was completed. Only dessert was left and that was already prepared. I knew the Anis Crème Brûlée would be an ideal ending with the Sauternes. He had fulfilled his obligation and was ready to sit among the honored guests and act accordingly. He started at once. As soon as he was handed the '49 Pichon, he began to preach how it was nice, but it could never fully compliment the great cheeses he had chosen for the conclusion to the main courses. "No meal is complete without a proper cheese course," he boldly stated.

I was not embarrassed. I was instantly able to perceive the aged aromas of tobacco and leather. The Pichon was a masterpiece and would, I thought, go very nicely with all three cheeses. It had been decanted cleanly and with impeccable storage, it was showing at its best.

"Ah," sighed Chef d'Larnio," I hope you all enjoyed yourself as much as I enjoyed working for you. Dessert will be served shortly and afterwards, you'll all have a rare freshly ground coffee, but I unfortunately have to leave immediately for New York. I have a morning television interview and as much as I hate to leave this simple but pleasant wine, I must be fresh for my adoring fans."

He looked at me and continued to be superior in his

attitude. "Thank you for sharing a humble but enjoyable Burgundy," he said.

After two years I still remember the rest of that day and I smile with conquest. Burgundy indeed! All I had heard about this pompous chef seemed to be true. Every time I open a bottle of a second growth Grand Cru Bordeaux, I retell this story.

The Thousand and Second Night

To the translating skills of Richard F. Burton

It was the day of their wedding and the young prince wanted the celebration to be held in the city of Shiraz in the heart of the desert. His father was pleased; his son would finally be married so he prepared a grand banquet for all of his Baghdad friends and worthy associates. Many, however, were using the caravan to Shiraz as an excuse for missing the gala event when in reality, it was their contempt for the young prince Shahryar that really made them decline the invitations.

A great array of food and wines were being prepared. Gifts, really meant to impress the father, were sent to Scheherazade and Shahryar. If they did not attend the wedding party, their token gifts might be seen as a gesture of compliance.

One large ebony box was carried to Shiraz with instructions that it be opened at the wedding reception. The ebony container was large enough to enclose a large sheep dog and was carved with rows of rose petals all around the upper section. The sachet itself was worth more than a thousand *mithkáls* of gold. Around the latches were carved clusters of grapes and chalices. Shahryar would have peeked to see its contents, being impetuous, if Aladdin Baba had not insisted that he follow the instructions saying that to ignore the request would be a foreboding omen prior to his wedding and since Aladdin Baba was his betrothed's personal aide, he complied.

The famous cleric Khayyám was coming from Naishápúr to perform and sanction the wedding. He had preached that evil begets evil and was not pleased that the sovereign had permitted Shahryar so many immoralities and injustices over the past months and years. It was the new *Jaláli* era renamed from *Jalál-ud-din*, which was one of the king's names and all the clerics were praying for an age of justice, tolerance and morality. Past sins were to be forgiven no matter how vicious or decadent. Many disagreed with this dictum but all vowed to follow the new rules, even Scheherazade who had seen first-hand the evils of the present kingdom and even the deeds of her betrothed. She had written a *Rubáiyát* as a gift to her husband to-be:

> *Of all the people in my life I've loved,*
> *There's one alone who soars just like a dove*
> *And he alone I never will forget.*
> *So, in pursuit of love my heart is moved.*

However, she kept the final draft of the *Rubáiyát* until the day of the wedding.

The noble lineage arrived the day before the wedding and all of Shiraz was excited. Extra money was to be made, as caterers would hire extra staff. More carriage drivers were to be needed for certain. Everyone expected thousands to arrive the following day but by noon on the day of the wedding, fewer than a hundred guests entered the town. The great hall was already filled with a thousand gifts including the ebony box, silks and woolen garments, rare spices and herbs, jewels and golden bracelets as well as coveted cheeses and clay carafes of deep garnet wine.

The Prince's father called the cleric to conference and asked for an explanation as to why so many of his invited guests were absent. The wise cleric chose his words carefully and told the king that for the past one thousand days, the Prince had been sadistic in seeking his pleasures from not only the palace harem, but also from the young ladies of Baghdad. He had so many sold off into slavery that the others rejoiced when they learned they were to be killed thus quickly ending a lifetime of pain and insult.

The king said that he knew of a few incidents where the females were found to be unworthy of nobility, but he had no idea that the carnage had been continued for so long. He was embarrassed about his son but forgiving at the same time. He told the cleric that he has, at last, found someone who can equally return his love, someone who will write poetry for him, share his good and bad times and who will give him legitimate heirs, and since so many gifts had already arrived, the king told the cleric to commence with the wedding because the new *Jaláli* age demanded that all begin anew and all the past forgiven.

Shahryar's father also told the servants to prepare the food and to bring out only the finest wines since much less would be needed. White wines had been received from Greece and ink-blue wines from the Etruscans' lands were readied. Shahryar would be their next sovereign and he will satisfy the requests of the powerful by ranking the importance of their wedding gifts. Of course, he would reward, most of all, those who attended the wedding. Knowing the prince favored the ebony box the most, the king inquired as to who had it delivered and was very pleased to learn it came from his new daughter-in-law, Scheherazade.

When the trumpets blew to beckon all to the wedding, Scheherazade called Aladdin Baba and asked if the ebony box had arrived and been sent to the reception hall where it might be the last gift to be opened. When she learned that her request had been fulfilled, she gave her personal aide another *Rubáiyát* and instructed him to give it to the prince immediately after he opened the box of ebony. It would be the largest gift that the prince would receive. It would sit ominous but stately in the wedding hall until the ceremony was completed.

The ceremony was much simpler and shorter than in years past. The new *Jaláli* demanded more simplicity as well as more honesty and forgiveness. All were amazed at how stoic the bride was during the blessing, even while they first danced and especially while Shahryar opened the many gifts.

Even though there was ample wine, as the gala neared its conclusion, Aladdin Baba brought a special carafe that Scheherazade requested to personally serve her new husband. She told him it was the finest of all the Shiraz wines available and that he should drink robustly and then make a toast to his future. He did. Then, with glee, he asked for the ebony box and asked who had sent it so his name could be added to the ledger his father told him to keep for granting future favors. Aladdin Baba announced that it was from his new wife as he translated the ancient Persian inscribed among the delicately carved roses. "A loaf of bread, a jug of wine and thou should have been all anyone ever need to spend a happy life." These were the words of Scheherazade's older sister to the prince.

"Open your gift," she told him. The excited, but no longer sober, Shahrya quickly opened the ebony box and retreated in horror to see the decapitated and amputated body of one of his former harem victims. He fell choking to his knees holding both his stomach and his throat.

"I will read to you the honest *Rubáiyát* that this new age of *Jaláji* requires," Scheherazade sang out:

> *Of all the people in my life I've loved,*
> *There's one alone who soars just like the dove.*
> *And she alone I never will forget:*
> *The sister you abused before you moved!*

"The Shiraz is poisoned," she whispered, "and after a thousand and one nights, on this thousand and second night, you've gotten your final reward."

The French Café

With respect for Ernest Hemmingway

There were few places left where an old man could sit and gather his thoughts over a glass of Beaujolais. It was past midnight. The young couple that owned the bistro was tired. Beaune is always a quiet town except during the harvest. Tourist visit to see the hospital, sample some Burgundies or use the village as a stopover. Most people had more important places to see. The young man opened a newly released Beaujolais-Villages and poured some into the old man's glass. He didn't pour as much into the glass as the old man would have poured himself, but the old man said nothing.

"Would you rather have a Côte de Beaune?"

The old man shook his head and sipped the wine.

"I have a Brouilly open and a Moulin-à-Vent. If I can't sell a real Burgundy, at least try the Moulin."

"I once drank an entire bottle of Chénas," said the old man. "It was twenty years ago but I remember it."

"Then you'd love a Côte de Beaune. It doesn't cost that much more."

The young man's wife came and wiped the table around the dish of cheese and the wine glass. She said nothing. As she walked back to the little bar, her husband watched the sway of her hips and the old man watched her long chestnut-brown hair bounce in the middle of her back. She turned off two of the four small lights above the bar and said that it was late and getting cold outside.

The old man smiled slightly and picked up a piece of cheese and held it under his nose. He lowered his hand, sipped some of the wine and raised his hand and smelled the cheese again before taking a small bite. He chewed slowly. Then he sipped a little more wine with some cheese still in his mouth while sucking some air between his lips. He could see the waiters from the café across the street leaving for the night. A woman with a long topcoat came to the window and peeked in for a second. She turned to his left and disappeared into the dark. The waiters shouted something to her that she ignored. She came back to the window again and the old man could see her short purple skirt because the topcoat was now partly unbuttoned.

The young couple wiped and cleaned around the bar without saying anything. The old man was now looking at the bar but did not seem to notice the bottles of Mommessin, Louis Jadot or Joseph Drouhin. He was dreaming of something in the past. He never thought of tomorrow and seldom thought about today. He did not turn his head toward the outside woman even when she scratched the nails of her right hand on the window, then turned and walked to the right this time continuing down the darkened street until she was invisible. Inside the now dim café, the wife looked quickly at the old man's wine glass expecting it to be near empty and mumbled to her husband that she knew the old man didn't have much money, was living alone and seldom spoke. "I wish he'd at least order a good Burgundy once in a while. Not so much that he'd spend more. I want him to experience a flavor, a taste near to heaven."

"You love wine too much," said her husband.

"No. Every time he comes here, it's near closing. He lives alone now since his wife died. I think he misses her too much to live."

"How do you know all this?"

"*Je ne sais pas.* He lives above the cheese merchant. He talked about him the last time I saw him here. He wasn't born in France, but his wife was." She talked as she put the last glasses away and cleaned the three remaining cheese dishes left on the small bar. "I never know how to act with him or what to say to him." She stopped cleaning and stared at the old man while he stared at the street beyond the window. Her frown relaxed. Her sleepy eyes opened more brightly.

"Say nothing unless he asks for something," the husband said as he walked back to the old man with the Beaujolais bottle. "Here." he said, "There's only a small pour remaining. Finish it before you go. It's late. While you sleep tomorrow, we have to open this place for Burgundy lovers."

The wife stared at her husband with disdain. He'll leave soon enough, she thought. He doesn't bother anyone. He likes that table because he can watch the people passing by in the night. Beaune has no big-city nightlife. She knew her husband wanted only to close the wine bar and get into bed with her for the night. The old man would have no one to hold or even talk to until he decided to return to the young couple's place tomorrow evening. The old man finished his wine, placed some Euros on the table and began to rise when he smiled at the husband as a way of thanking him for the last free pour of Beaujolais. The wife hurried ahead of the old man to open the door for him as he wrapped his scarf around his neck then faced the wind in the street. He walked slowly toward the Hospices de Beaune that was near the cheese merchant and then was out of sight.

She closed the door stopping the French wind. She took her husband's hand. "Some day when you're very old," she said, "someone will offer you a glass of nice Beaujolais or maybe some very good Burgundy for no reason at all." She smiled, then walked to the bar and continued to clean the remaining wine glasses. As she was putting off the lights, her husband opened and poured some Aloxe-Corton into two glasses. He sat where the old man had been sitting and called her to join him for a minute before they left. I will have some of this left for tomorrow, he thought to himself.

"I saw you give him a smile. A grin. A smile of encouragement."

"What else has he?" she answered. "Fifty years from now will you need a smile from someone?

"When I saw how you wanted him to be happy as I wanted him to leave, I thought there might be other things I still have not learned from you." I'll open the Corton, he mused. She deserves it and if not now, when? They clinked their glasses together. "Look how late it is. Today has already become yesterday and it's dark and cold."

"*En automne, et aussi au printemps, il fait frais à Beaune,*" she softly said.

A single dim light burned on and sitting with her husband, she smelled the Burgundy. She sipped it. She took another larger sip and smiled just as she had done before.

Tomorrow, God willing, the old man will smile too, she thought.

The Wedding Feast

John, Chapter 2. Thank you.

It was staged as the biggest wedding the town ever had and it proved to be true. The family from the carpenter shop, the baker's family, even ranchers and farmers from all around the town were invited. There would be plenty of food and lots of wine to drink so everyone showed up.

Ester and James were friends of the bride and Ester was part of the wedding. James worked as a caterer and volunteered to help with the reception party. He had the experience of tasting many fine wines, interesting types of food, and had experienced many more social events than Ester. She considered herself just an average girl. She was healthy, well kept and strong and would make a good mother and wife. Ester did not mind hard work and knew that her life with James was a blessing. She was happy to be in the wedding and glad to feel a little important, at least for one day. While she marched into the entrance, stood with the bride as they approached the Rabbi, and was responsible for many little details as they all gathered for the reception, she felt needed and important.

Ester told James to bring out carafes of their best wine to serve and she made sure everyone could sample the fig and sheep cheese appetizers. She frequently told the bride that everyone was enjoying himself or herself and that she was the most beautiful bride they'd ever seen. James told the new husband that many of the richer guests complimented him on the wine and food and then he told the same thing to the parents of both the bride and the groom.

Music began, more food was served and soon both the richer and the poorer people from the town were praising the father of the bride and toasting blessings for the new couple. Grilled vegetables and roasted racks of lamb seem to come out of the kitchen as frequently as a fly or as fast as an ant attacks your outside summer lunch. The more people danced, the more they drank and after the best man toasted the new couple, James brought new carafes of wines imported for this very special occasion. This was indeed, the biggest and best wedding this community had ever seen. A sheepherder was heard to praise the lamb as the best he'd ever eaten. The mason and carpenter sat together drinking for a while as their wives fed the many children who also attended the wedding. It was good, they thought, for the children to see the adults at play and maybe even be helpful if necessary.

The bride's father, who was close friends with the carpenter's wife, told her that he would be helping the new couple financially when they decided to build a new place of their own and that her husband and son should begin thinking of designing a new set of blueprints because, of course, they would get the job to build the new place. The wife smiled and told him that he had always done so much for her family and even when they were children playing together, he had always watched out for her. "When I met Joe, you were so happy for me," she told him.

"And I still am," he responded. "Your family has never had it easy but all three of you are among the most sincere people in this town. Remember, your mother and my mother were friends. Friends help each other."

He was called to dance with his daughter and everyone raised their glasses to salute his generosity. Hummus was served on soft bread slices and more wine was called for as even the oldest members of the party began to drink and dance.

James had been so busy helping direct the wine and food service that he had not yet danced with Ester who had also been busy trying her best to make the bride relax and enjoy this special day. No one seemed to notice that the last selection of wines was thinner and dull or that the most recent course of food was mostly over cooked.

While James was talking with Joe, Joe's wife and Ester both heard them discuss how this last course was over-cooked and that the wine now had a hint of vinegar. Nothing else was said about it. Joe asked to dance with Ester and his wife went to talk with her son about helping. James went to tell the cooks to be more careful and not over-cook the next racks. He then went looking for more carafes of wine but found only ceramic water jugs similar to the ones he used to carry water to the summer workers who stayed in the field all day. He opened one so he could take Ester a refreshing drink and was surprised to see that it was filled with wine.

He refilled his own glass and began to serve all the other guests with empty glasses. He took one sip and then another and thought, I must have had a bad jug before. As he realized how good the newly found wine was, he noticed that all the guests were smiling and talking about how the host had saved the best for last! New racks of lamb were served, deliciously moist and spiced and the best wine of the reception enhanced the food. No one had ever been to a party like this where the final offerings were the best of the evening.

Ester ran to James to tell him how pleased the bride and groom were and how all the guests were complimenting her on arranging a great event. The carpenter, his wife and son left soon after this course was served but not before the bride's father said, "I can never thank you enough for attending our wedding and reception." A few of the local businessmen and a couple of farmers also were leaving and they told the bride's father that they had never enjoyed such good food and great wine and that no one had ever saved the best for last. Even the Rabbi told them that he was amazed to have had the best and greatest wine last. "Even with most guests here a little, well, intoxicated, they could still tell that it was the greatest vintage they'd ever experienced," he said.

"This was a wedding they'll talk about for years," Ester told James as they shook hands with Joe, his wife and son and said, "Goodbye."

The Hunting Camp

A Zane Grey Perspective

Just as in "Tige's Lion", I too have a tale to tell that is a bit different. A hunting trip through the west would involve tumbleweeds, cottonwoods, horses and vast open spaces with the stalking of big game beneath the golden sunsets amongst the purple sage. However, when three colleagues and I made a pursuit of moose deep in the north west forests of Maine, we were not skilled cowboys nor plainsmen. We loved the idea of the adventure, but were old enough to have gotten very used to refined sleeping accommodations and culinary comforts.

We all enjoyed a glass of good wine with dinner. We all like to shoot skeet, hunt and fish. We all decided to combine shooting and tracking with good wine and excellent dining while on the hunt. We would hunt each day, and then retire to a lodge at a campsite deep in the Maine woods to eat and sleep. Three nights would require six bottles of wine. Tom brought a 1988 Chateau Beychevelle and a nice Gevrey-Chambertin. I had a 1990 Prunotto Barolo and a Brusco dei Barbi Brunello di Montalcino and a Kenwood Artist Series 1985 Cabernet Sauvignon while Joseph overwhelmed us with a 1997 Tignanello from Tuscany's Antinori family and from a simple brown paper bag, he withdrew a Chateau Latour from 1961.

We knew all the wines promised a great experience but were star-struck, as we stood speechless staring at the Latour.

Tom Gilman had been hunting for decades and had made the arrangements for the local guide, the lodge and had even found a grocery store where we bought all the requirements to pair with great wines. Joseph too, was a good hunter. I hadn't traveled as many times on hunting trips as my two friends but I did hunt as often as possible for both small game, birds and deer. Moose would be a bit more exciting. We would share two bottles each night after hunting. With seven very interesting red wines to choose from, we'd save the odd number for a hunting celebration toast.

The guide, Hector, never told us his last name but explained everything else. He knew the area and he knew the nature of moose. Hector knew the land very well and promised us that because of the light early snow, we'd be able to track our game easily when necessary but for the first day, we'd be placed along known moose paths. So, on the morning of December 3rd, he routed us from our sleep at five o'clock, which is what he did every morning anyway, asked Joseph to rake over the hot coals in the Franklin stove, pointed out that there was an additional thick frost on the snow cover, guided us toward already-made pancakes and suggested we move quickly.

"God, it's cold!" exclaimed Tom. It was twenty-two degrees.

Hector smiled and I moved closer to Joseph at the stove and dressed as quickly as possible. Joseph was dressed already and began eating as he checked the wine bottles that were lined up like soldiers on the uppermost cabin shelf opposite the Franklin stove wall. He had already decided to open the Barolo I brought along with Tom's 2002 Gevrey-

Chambertin from Louis Latour with that night's first-full-day meal after hunting. With luck, we might have a sliver of moose tenderloin to roast with the beef and polenta that we brought with us.

Hounds may have helped in that remote section of Western Maine near the Canadian border but our more modern style of hunting was to sit and wait along a trail where moose were known to travel. It was ten degrees below freezing when we were all placed by our guide on a trail heading toward an open meadow section of the hillside. At seven o'clock, the sun had just begun warming things when Tom's shot rang out. Two more shots followed making me wonder if he had a clean kill or were the extra shots taken in frustration as the moose ran away? By the time I climbed down from my tree roost and got down the trail, Joseph, Tom and Hector were cleaning the first kill and preparing to make the trek back to the lodge. The area had been disturbed with human activity and we knew nothing would enter our hunting zone until much later that afternoon or early evening.

It took us to nearly eleven that morning to warm up, dry our gear and then, after lunch, we set the table for dinner, pulled the corks on the Barolo and the Burgundy and then headed out for the late afternoon hunt. I was glad no one saw anything because I knew the polenta would taste like a millionaire's dish instead of a peasant's meal when paired with two great red wines. We were warm again, had a moose, albeit a small female, and listened to Hector's talk of other less cultured hunters while we dined.

The Côte d'Or makes great pinot noirs and the '02 was a special treat. I explained to Hector that the wines were named after the towns they came from but certain single vineyards were very famous so the towns, back in the late 19th century, changed their names by adding the vineyard name to the town, thus changing the village of Gevrey to Gevrey-Chambertin. Adding the Grand Cur vineyard name of Le Chambertin to the village, made it easier to sell their wine. The town of Chambolle did the same thing with the Musigny vineyard. Tom had tasted a 1995 Chambolle-Musigny just a week before our hunting adventure. We all loved Côte d' Or wines and this red from the Côte de Nuits was beautiful with the beef. The Barolo was bigger, had great rose petal and sweet road-tar aromas and converted the simple polenta into a dish for a king. Moose hunting was great. Louis Latour knew Burgundy, Prunotto knew Barolo and Hector knew moose.

The next day, December 4th, began at five again and while we dressed we listened to the wind-blown snow as it fell. It had warmed up five degrees but was snowing and made expectations for another successful hunt look bleak. As we were about to leave, Joseph asked if he should decant the '97 Tignanello before we left. I rejoiced with exhilaration at the thought of an older wine but we decided to hunt successfully first, then properly serve the classic Italian red. Wine lovers become familiar with key aromas and sportsmen are familiar with the pungent animal odor. With big game – it gets easy.

We were all seated in new locations that Hector had chosen and in a flash the scene changed. The snow stopped. The sun broke through the overcast. Joseph saw two moose heading toward him.

"I fingered the safety," Joseph said, "I never sat so still as

I watched both brown monsters approach. I knew they'd be heading for the river's edge where they could scrap through the snow to get at some grass and when they came into range, they began to walk in single file giving me the choice of either one. The second moose seemed to have a larger rack even though they were about the same size." It took three shots to drop the target and when we all got to the kill, Joseph had started to field clean the moose before Hector even got there. He and our guide would pole sled the animal back toward our lodge while Tom and I went back to hunt out the morning. Joseph finished telling us about the kill but we felt it had all happened too quickly. By eleven, the weather abruptly changed once again with more snow falling and chilly winds biting through our clothes. We knew the forecast was good for the 5th, so we retired for the day and began to think about the Tignanello. It's amazing what you can put up with outside when you know what's waiting for you inside. That's the lure of great wines.

Back at the cabin, Hector was preparing a late afternoon dinner so we could all get to sleep early. I knew it just had to be my turn next so I didn't mind the very early dinner because I'd be up before five the next day. Joseph had already opened and decanted the 1988 Beychevelle for the contrast wine. I suggested we also drink the 1985 Kenwood Cabernet Sauvignon as a contrast flavor and compare it to the French Bordeaux. With baked potatoes, sautéed mushrooms and steak; all three wines would marry well with the meat. Which one would enhance the food best was to be our consideration. The '85 Artist Series had some merlot and cab franc in it like the Bordeaux. Ever since 1971, Tignanello's first vintage, the wine used cabernet sauvignon to deepen the sangiovese. The hunting was so successful, we thought we should celebrate now with the extra wine.

"I can see what you mean about enjoying the smell," said Hector. He drank more slowly on the second night.

The guide, Joseph and I voted for the Tignanello as the best example, but Tom thought the Beychevelle was the culinary champion with that meal. We all enjoyed my Kenwood but thought it may have peaked in complexity a few years ago. "Maybe we should have kept the Beychevelle as a contrast to tomorrow's Latour," Joseph said, but I disagreed.

"A 1961 Chateau Latour should have nothing to disturb it. I've had a few other '61's from Bordeaux, but never the Latour. If we're lucky tomorrow, we'll have completed the greatest hunting and dining adventure ever. It will call for something special."

Joseph and Tom each had a moose and Hector said that the snow would bring more moose down the hillside toward the river and nearer to our cabin. We wouldn't have to travel far. I was excited. The only tragedy would be if I did not get to see anything. All three of us fell asleep talking about the nuance of cassis, leather and subtle tobacco exhibited in all three wines as they married with the sautéed wild mushrooms. Great friends – great food – and great wine. What an adventure!

December 5th, our last day to hunt, began at 4:15 A.M. Hector wanted us out and hidden before any moose began to move. It also would take almost an hour for our human scents to dissipate and make us completely stealthy. He placed me highest on the run. I'd get the first chance to see any moose moving down hill in search of food. As I watched the sun try to break through a lead, bullet-gray sky, I noticed some movement high on the hill. This will be the best day yet, I thought. As I, ever so slowly, moved to my left to better see what it was, the seat frame snapped and I saw a deer, not a moose moving as I started to fall. I pulled my rifle in tightly and bounced to a lower limb then quickly fell another eleven feet into a snowdrift beneath my tree. I was lucky I hadn't broken any bones. I was surprised how quiet the catastrophe was: a broken seat, a torn limb, lots of bark off one section of the tree and crushed underbrush beneath the snow. I was lucky.

I spent the next hour slowly walking downhill with a limp in my right leg toward Tom's location when I spotted a moose. It saw me too and jumped off the trail before I could even raise my rifle. This added insult to injury. I was sore, tired, angry, and now the snow that had gotten into my boots and jacket had melted from my body heat and the wet began to refreeze.

As I rounded the next turn, Tom stood there to meet me. "I saw you coming a mile back and came down to head up to help you begin gutting the moose, but I didn't hear any shots. Why are you limping?"

"I didn't shoot," I said. "I fell."

"Let's get you back to the cabin and make sure you're alright."

Joseph sent Hector back to stoke the fire at the lodge and we three trudged along, two of us happy that I was not killed in the fall and one sore and saddened with disappointment. I told them about the fall, the missed moose and the freezing water inside my clothes. They joked and said a good meal and a great wine will make it all fade away.

We were clean and warm by early evening. My arm and leg were still hurting but the thought of a 1961 Chateau Latour paired with a grilled rack of lamb took away some pain. Spending time hunting with your best friends in a countryside filled with scenic wonder, hearing the report of a rifle in freezing weather and taking a moose for meat and trophy is an adventure few get. Drinking a wine like the '61 Latour is an experience even fewer will ever have. We drank the Barbi Brunello as an aperitif.

Hector had the meal almost completed when Joseph pulled the cork and began to decant the historic Bordeaux. I silently wished we had kept the Beychevelle to use as a comparison, but after the day I'd had, I refused to linger on negative thoughts.

Joseph finished decanting and poured Tom the first glass as I took my seat. Tom swirled, sniffed, and looked at me with the sadness of a lonely cowboy and said, "The wine is corked. Totally corked."

To this day, I'm torn between missing the moose, falling from the hunting roost and the worst thing that could happen to the best of all wines, being corked. We left the hunting camp the next morning never to return to that part of the country again. Joseph and Tom would share their game and retell many times how they got it, but I kept the bad cork to help me remember the adventure.

Holy Smoke & Gee Wiz

Kurt Vonnegut, Jr.: prophet and philosopher

Before the New Ice Age had begun, in more optimistic times, when people stopped smoking cigarettes without the federal government prohibiting them, it was easier to find and purchase a rare artifact. People had more than 2 cars. Nearly everyone lived on a cul-de-sac with an Indian name and you would disqualify yourself from any desirable social group if you had more than 1 child. Bear with me. Cheap alcohol was low-class and marijuana was legal and boring so I sought out a rare bottle of old wine to share with a time-traveling friend of mine.

Most of northern Europe and all of Canada were evacuated to the south. We were running out of cul-de-sac communities and even worse, we were almost out of Indian names.

I was the youngest of 5 boys who all were sent to Iraq and Afghanistan and Syria to use up the products of the industrial military complex that President Eisenhower had warned us about. Sadly, 4 of us were killed. Not me. I spent most of my time serving generals some great examples of pinot noir from Oregon and New Zealand. No French example could be found anywhere after we banned all their products when they backed the 5th French Canadian revolt. I was also able to avoid destruction when we had to bomb ourselves, and the excrement hit the fan, to speed up the depilation of excess weapons so President Billy Pilgrim could announce growth in the economy. Now, after all those years serving good wines to less appreciative palates, I decided I wanted to savor the world's oldest bottle of, hopefully, a Romanée-Conti or at the very least, a Romanée-Saint-Vivant, even if I had to visit Tralfamadore to get it.

There's something magical about drinking an old wine that has been carefully stored. You drink history. You savor the sunshine and rain from the distant year. You don't chug; you sip and meditate with old wines.

Since China, Japan and Saudi Arabia owned everything in North America you would think those countries would be the places to begin the search. Not so. I say "not so" a lot, so bear with me. General Brendon used to say, "Isn't that what you told me yesterday, Flex?" and I'd answer, "Not so, sir." The general was a non-swearer, not religious, just a non-swearer and his influence started me calling wine drinkers who didn't swirl, sip or spit at tastings, just plain old wine anus-holes. The failure to write out numbers is a New Jersey public school matter all unto itself. Is it proper? Not so. So, I sat at the Internet for days, weeks and months searching for someplace or someone that might have really old wines. I did get over a dozen hits about Burgundy's (the wine region in France, not the color) old wines. I was corrected with the capitalization of the word internet by my computer's spell checker which seems to think it is a god, maybe it is someone's God? Not so, I'd say, but it did help. I got 7 sources for Romanée-Saint-Vivant and 2 for a Romanée-Conti. There were thousands of Burgundy-like wines from Oregon, California, Australia, New Zealand, Tasmania, Hungary and even Russia with 19 Chinese Burgundy-like wines from, as they said, any year you might need. Not so, I thought. They'll just print a label with the requested date and once you buy it and taste it and the excrement hits the fan, you're just excrement out of luck! The Chinese invented the slogan "Buyer Beware", not the Romans.

No, the best bet would be to find someone who kept their grandparents' wine collection hidden, after the government decided to tax everything you ever got from someone, deep in a cool slaughterhouse or in a cold old well.

My first quest was at a closing tavern in Athena, New York. The owner had a Picasso on the wall, the first player piano built in Rochester and a signed photograph of Atlantic City's first Miss America. It was thought he cellared other treasurers like old Burgundy and if there is a Devine Providence, one who still has all his followers still drinking wine today, an aged Romanée-Conti just might be included in his cellar.

"Hello," I said as I entered the Inn. "Are you Henry Bergeron?" I asked.

"I'm Henry Berger," he corrected me. "Are you the fellow who wants to buy the piano? Are you the player of pianos?"

"Not so," I quickly answered. "I'm the guy who called and asked about the old wines."

"All gone," he said. "Drank every gosh darn bottle myself. Sorry."

"Did you have any old French Burgundy?"

"I had cases and cases of them, not really old, a few from the 1940s, most from 1976 and '78, and a few from 2002, 2025 and 2061. All were delightful but nothing really old except maybe the few from the 1940s. I did know a woman," he added, "who had some Bordeaux from 1929. Forget Burgundy; look for Bordeaux."

We talked for a while about how cold it's gotten over the past decade and I learned that he was related to a former Miss America. He wanted to move to Saudi Arabia. "If I could travel back in time," he said, "I'd like to live just before the major recession that wiped out the middle class in America. I'd move to Atlantic City and open a restaurant that everyone could afford to go to and charge only retail prices for wines on my wine list."

Nice idea, I thought.

I told Henry that the only good thing the new Ice Age had done was preserve great old wines. I thanked him for the Bordeaux suggestion and told him to try to find someone who knew about Tralfamadore and suggested that when he did move to Atlantic City, he should open a sherry bar called *Cul*-de-*Sac* and have only Native Americans for bartenders.

"That's a great idea," he told me.

If it was Bordeaux I needed to seek out, I'd find the oldest wine from the Bordeaux region and maybe it might just be the oldest wine in the world. Back in the early 2000s, some people found 18th Century Champagne on a sunken boat that was still good, and in this century, 9 Italian Barolos that were over 120 years old were discovered beneath what used to be a place called the Sistine Chapel. Only one was worth drinking. Not so, I thought. Maybe they over-aired them before serving them was my consideration. "Not so," was what I told the New York City wine merchant who wanted me to invest in new Spanish whites. I told him that I believed all 9 bottles of the rare Barolo were good and yes, priceless, but were hidden again to avoid having people like me seeking them out. So, they reported that the wines were bad.

The very next day I read about a Prince from Saudi Arabia who had gotten some old wines from an island somewhere off England. There weren't many princes left nowadays. I recalled a photo of him with President Pilgrim when he had made a deal for us to buy sand from the Middle East. Since we made nothing in America except bad beer, cheap Bourbon and some short-lived wines from the island of Calioregon, which was formed after the really big quake, and since his fatherland owned nearly everything we had, we pretty much had to ignore the excrement hitting the economic fan and go along with buying the sand. Since he did not drink, at least in public, he featured his old wines as art objects and even had them shipped to international museums. I remembered telling Henry Berger how way too many wine collectors really urinated me off because they were more concerned with the outside label than what's inside the wine bottle. He really shocked me when he said, "Not so," and gave no further comments.

No one knew what had caused this New Ice Age but I decided to get to New York and seek out the Sheik's wine collection before the city was closed like Boston and Hartford had been because of the snow. I learned from a Tralfamadore day-tripper that all the ice was coming from some other type of ice and everything buried in it was preserved perfectly so if I could find an old bottle, even if it was 150 years old, it should still be good. He also told me that he had known President Pilgrim when he was a freshman at Yale; that's when there still was a Yale, and that

Billy liked really old Bordeaux even back then. They met when he asked Billy where he could get the same skull tattoo he saw on him while in the showers after lacrosse practice. It was he who had the Saudi Arabian collector host the international exhibition of ancient wines at the New York museum. As luck would have it, the city was put on notice to begin evacuation just as I arrived. I was getting sick of the excrement hitting the fan overtime. I made progress in my quest, and I knew I was near to my holy grail, so when I was told to pack up and leave the city with everyone else, I told the city official, "Not so." Queens and Brooklyn were already arctic wastelands so I had to work fast. Manhattan had always been a cold place for visitors, even during the summers back in the late 20th Century. But that was more of a social cold instead of a temperature cold.

My time-traveling friend told me that if I went back to yesterday with him, the museum would be empty at 9 o'clock in the morning and together we would scour the ancient wine collection. We did. We got there yesterday. When we arrived, we went straight to the basement where parts of the exhibition were still being packed for shipping back to the Middle East. There were wines everywhere. Yes! There was a full case of Romanée-Conti from two centuries ago with vintage dates just after the last war ever fought with pride and dignity, the 2nd Big One.

Even better, there was a crate with bottles of Chateau Margaux from the 1860s and 2 bottles of Chateau Haut-Brion from 1797. I thought they were empty at first; not so. Both bottles have to be the oldest bottles of wine in the world and they were still filled.

"A dream come true!" I exclaimed to my friend from

Tralfamadore. "Holy Smoke. This could be it." My friend, who had only recently come to like wine and got to savor it only when his time traveling brought him back to Earth during these past 3 centuries, still preferred Tralfamadorian mineral water. "Gee wiz," he answered. He, not I, had gotten to taste some wine at a wedding in Israel once that he said was quite good, but that was during a time-warp-trip over 22 centuries ago. "The wines kept getting better and better as the wedding party went on," he said.

I took 2 large glasses from a display and withdrew my non-powered corkscrew. I inserted it and withdrew the cork. I slowly poured the oldest wine in the world into my glass but only powdery ice crystals flowed out. The wine had been super-chilled. Both bottles were the same and as the crystals of ice touched the glass, it too froze along with the table the glasses were on. My friend and I departed for a far distant past before we were also frozen like the oldest wine in the world.

The excrement really hit the fan this time because it would now be getting colder faster than people could move away from it. I knew the Sheik has sought out the best cellar condition for aging his priceless wine collection but whatever his cellar master had decided to use for a cellar will end up perfectly aging everything. Will his wines be saved and aged for future drinkers, I thought? Not so, I decided.

An Adventure of Ted Reywas

Inspired by Samuel. Yes, Mark Twain.

Aunt May lived with her dead sister's son on the edge of town near the river. He and his best friends were good boys who had possibly heard too many *Treasure Island* or *Robinson Crusoe* stories.

"Teddy."

There was no response.

"Teddy!"

"Just a minute Aunty May."

"Ted Reywas! I have chores for you."

That boy, she thought, God love him, can't help if he's filled with Old Scratch, but he's my sister's only siblin' and with his Ma and Pa both done gone, well, he'll be the ruination of me before I can bring myself to punish him the way he needs to be punished. He is obedient. He does add a sunny ray to my gloomy days, she said to herself many times. However, there's way too much circumstantial evidence time and time again that his cunning and mysterious nature has and will again lead him to some dangerous exploit for which I should be responsible.

"Aunty May, me and Foxey is heading to the docks today to watch dem build da new pier. We'll be back 'fore dark." He was off running, still barefoot, before she could answer him.

"I'z sees you later, Miz May," Foxey shouted as they ran off. "Teddy, wez headin' down ta da river and da caves, kay?"

"Let's be pirates, Foxey."

"Ole man Tugman ain't makin' moonshine no more, so let's go see da ole still."

"Wellin…"

"If''n you don't, pirates is good, but I'z sure likes da smell down der."

"Let's go then. Long as I'm back 'fore dark, Aunty May won't worry none."

Two would-be pirates scurried from the riverbank toward the wooded hillside and as they always wanted another adventure, they immediately planned to sip some of a jug as soon as they found one with its illegal contents. It wasn't the moonshine that created an adventure; it was the knowledge that Treasury officials were always on the hunt for these lawbreakers. Ted had had some blackberry brandy once because of a serious cold and at the time he wondered why in the world anyone would drink whiskey without the sugary blackberry syrup.

Foxey had tasted whiskey lots of time while trying to show his stepfather that he too could be a man. It seemed common that all the young country boys assumed that whiskey drinking was what it took to be a man.

Nearly two miles into the woods along side a small offshoot of the river was the abandoned still. The two boys got there quickly. As they approached, they pretended to be local moonshiners sleuthing about and watching for Treasury Agents.

"Smell dat, Teddy?"

"Smells good don't it?" answered Ted even though he had not the practice Foxey had at picking up the aromas of corn mash and distillate vapors. But he had learned very early in the schoolyard games that when you're pretending anything you have to pretend everything.

The old shed was nearly overgrown with swamp moss and the nearby jagged rocky ledges were filled with small caves where, during extremely cold winters, bears hibernated. Ted and Foxey had been told over and over again from the time they were old enough to walk out alone and play in the nearby yards to stay away from the caves because of the bears.

"You'd make fine bear food," Aunt May had said to instill a sense of fright in them. "Teddy, they'd have ya fur lunch and then et your playmate fur dinner."

Both boys were thinking back to their childhood warnings as they quietly surveyed the old still hoping to find some moonshine. They pulled an old crate from the bottom of a barrel rack, opened it and saw a collection of empty bottles. Foxey tossed one bottle into the nearby opening of a small cave and was excited to hear the echo of the shattering glass reverberate in the stone cave. "Hear dat, Teddy?"

Ted threw the second bottle but he hit the edge of the opening and shattered light green glass all along the wall of rock. "Give me 'nother, Foxey. Let me try 'gain."

In less time than you can say Jackie Robinson, the boys smashed a dozen and a half bottles against the rock and into the cave opening. As they reached the bottom row of bottles, they were shocked to lift a full one. *"...ia Dare"* was all that was left of the label and Foxey quickly broke off the top releasing the intoxicating genii of Scuppernong. The sweet aromas danced in his nose. He smiled. Slowly, he sipped some of the nectar and then he chugged it. Ted grasped the bottle and also chugged. Both boys remained standing until the bottle was empty. The sweet syrupy wine enticed them into gluttons for the alcohol.

The moonshine wine was gone and so were their wits. They fell asleep.

Scuppernong had done in stronger men than Foxey and Ted. Scuppernong was the greenish-yellow superstar of the bronzed-skinned, sugar-laden Muscadine grapes belonging to the *Vitis rotundifolia* species. Years earlier, old man Tugman used to sing out, "Der's gold in dem der hills," but few knew he was talking about the fermented grape product that produced a strong-scented dark golden sweet wine. Its aroma is so strong that when mixed with Concord or Catawba, it would overwhelm the Labrusca scent we call foxy. A Scuppernong blend was the base of the famous Virginia Dare that was the best-selling American wine for two full decades before Prohibition cursed the nation.

By midnight, Aunt May was furious, then disgusted and finally frightened to death. She knew the two boys had gone off into the woods along side the bear caves near the river. Had they drowned, she thought, No, they could both swim. Had they been abducted? Had they been hurt and unable to walk back to the village? No. Had the bears gotten th… "Oh God," she screamed. "They bin et by da bears!"

Aunt May put on her ragged work jacket, the one she only wore when working in her vegetable garden, and ran to the county sheriff's office. She wanted to run quickly but she was old and simply had to meander like a widow. You don't know anythin' 'bout me lessen you read a book 'bout the South, she thought as she waddled along and rehearsed what she'd say to the sheriff. Her boy was dead…et by a bear, and his best friend, dat poor boy Foxey, was dead too. Oh God, what a horrible death! I knew I should never have let them go wanderin' into the woods like some Davey Crockett.

By sunrise, the two young adventurers had woken up and looked at each other with a desert thirst and a vomit tongue.

"Pooty soon I'z be a-shou'n' fo help," said Foxey. "Ole man Tugman ain't made dat stuff! Too easy ta drink!"

Teddy answered by telling Foxey that Mr. Tugman was known for making the smoothest moonshine in the county but they must have been drinking some kind of wine.

"God, Foxey, we been here all night. It's light outside now. Aunty May's a gonna kill us... me at least."

The two hung-over young drunks waddled to the entrance and stared into the wilderness. One full-grown bear was grazing for berries near the edge of the river, just beyond the trees. "Don't move," said Ted.

In the mean time, Aunt May had the sheriff and both his deputies scouring the riverside looking for bodies. They assumed that even if bears had gotten them, they'd find parts of them with pants and shoes still on. If they drowned, they'd have to look further down stream for the next few days waiting for the bodies to fill with gas and rise to the surface. All three walked together, slowly, into the woods toward the hill slopes where bears were known to hibernate, an isolated place not far from the unknown moon-shiner shack of old man Tugman.

"Lookie here," shouted the sheriff as he approached the bear cave. Broken bottles were everywhere. "Da boys musta tried to scare dem off. It musta bin some fight! See any body parts?" he called to the deputies.

They went no further, assuming no need to look any deeper into the woods, so they never found Tugman's moonshine establishment or the hung-over boys. Aunt May's hysteria had dominated their thoughts, and they too, easily believed that bears had eaten the boys. They retreated toward the river and returned to town with the gruesome news that poor Ted Reywas and his friend Foxey were dead.

Aunt May cried out saying that she was responsible and that the two boys were good boys and that she would never forgive herself for being so strict with them that they had to sneak away. The sheriff said he'd help her to the church so they could make arrangements.

Back at Tugman's still, the boys stood facing a real bear. Foxey, slowly reach for a half-filled broken bottle of the Devil's golden liquid and rolled it toward the bear. The bear rose up, stared, then smelled and licked the puddle of Scuppernong. He licked more. The boys smiled and Teddy said, "Dat bear don't know how bad he's a gonna feel later on."

Shortly, the bear wandered toward the river obviously needing some cool water to refresh his mouth and stomach. The boys slowly began to make their way back toward the village discussing what story they could tell Aunt May for having been out all night.

"Da truth ain't never worked by me," said Foxey.

"Well," said Teddy, "I can't seem ta make up no story no better dan da real one. You feelin' any better yit, Foxey? A while ago, you was talking like da farm workers."

"No way. Teddy, I'z still sick."

"Well, yoz speakin' better. Let's git on home."

The two young boys slowly approached Aunt May's house from the back yard just as she was returning from the church and entering the front door. She was still weeping as she entered the house and stopped dead still as she heard the back door close.

"Aunty May. Aunty May."

The tearful woman thought that it sounded like Teddy but she knew better. However, she was willing to see even a ghost if she could tell it her last goodbyes and share final thoughts about how she loved him.

"Let's git, Teddy," said Foxey. "Iz need some sarsaparilla bad."

Aunt May knew that voice was Teddy's friend, Foxey. She darted toward the back summer-kitchen and walked in just as both boys were about to leave and find someplace where they could concoct a better story about staying out all night.

"Great God Almighty!" exclaimed Aunt May. "You... You're flesh and bones...you're both here...you're both alive."

"I'm rottin' glad I iz," Foxey said slowly. "I'm gonna run on and..." but before he could step to the door Aunt May grabbed them both and squeezed them harder than they've ever been squeezed. Her tearful face was wiped dry on the cheeks of Teddy. "I was plannin' a funeral and now, thank God Almighty, I got to plan a party," she said.

The boys began to relax a bit and Aunt May made them sit down for blueberry biscuits and melted butter. Before she could ask them where they'd been or what happened, she told them about all that happened in town during the night. She told how the Lakeland boy lost control of his run-away horse and wagon and how it ripped right through the newly painted fence that was done by the neighbor's boy and then how the run-away carriage knocked over the kerosene can at the general store which led to the fire and how all the people had to gather to fight the fire. Aunt May said that it was the most exciting night ever for the small riverside village and nothing in history or ever again would anyone see so much action.

"It wasn't until 'bout midnight that I even knowed you was missing," she told Teddy.

"God!" shouted Foxey, "and we wuz out and missed da most citin' thing ever happen here."

"We went lookin' for adventure. See pirates or somethin' and all we did was sleep right through the best night ever," Teddy answered.

Aunt May told the boys how the sheriff saw all the broken glass at the mouth of the cave and the bear prints in some mud and figured they'd tried their best to fight off the bears before they got eaten.

Both Teddy and Foxey then told her the full truth about how they found the old abandoned still and that no moonshine was left. They did admit to sampling some golden grape juice that was still sweeter than anything they'd ever had and how, like Goldilocks, it put them both to sleep until sunrise.

"I promise, Aunty May, I'll never drink that *Dare* stuff again."

Foxey too pledged to keep away from any spirits whether they were found in a bottle or in a graveyard and Aunt May promised to let Foxey stay with them whenever he cared to spend time with his best friend, Teddy.

The Wake

With humble apologies to James Joyce

Sean slid his chair closer to the table as his friends raised their glasses to make a reluctant toast to the upcoming winter holiday. Semester exams had been difficult; winter had arrived, and a death had made it even more dreary.

—Wine is food. It's the liquid part of the meal and just as we tire of the same foods served way too often, wine also can become tedious, said Sean. He thought to himself for a second about how wine had changed his life. He'd begun to seek more enjoyment and ignore the guilt of sin; so many things were sin, all of which had been drilled into him since his first day at Clongowes School as a child.

—We all seek new adventures, new movies, travels, books, songs, and even meeting new people. It's change that makes life more exciting. Why then do so many of us continue to drink the same old wines when there are thousands of different taste experiences waiting to excite us? Sean asked. Liam, you have to make an effort to live to the fullest. Remember, as Aquinas said, *"Bonum est in quod tendit appetitus."* He used his Latin as if he were at a workbench hammering out a word. The night before, they had all been to the Wake of an admired literature professor with whom they had shared both wine and conversation outside of class. They were troubled that his life had come to an end while he was still young. It was he who had taught them that wine was civilization's companion. Seeing him lying there, dead, had changed them all.

Lynch and Liam looked to the older Stephen for worldly advice; seldom did they appeal to Sean or his drinking buddy, Gabriel Doyle, but it was near Christmas and all the University students were heading home for the winter holidays and, as usual, many of them met in the Commons Hall Entertaining Room to discuss the semester's classes, Irish history, or how they had switched from drinking Guinness Black Lager to wine. Liam Conroy thought it the grandest epiphany in his life when he first learned each grape makes an entirely different wine. Lynch still drank only Johnny Powers and Guinness, but once in a while, very seldom, he drank Claret.

—Good is that which we desire? Stephen translated Sean's Latin with a questioning look.

—Have you tried Portuguese verdelho instead of the very watered-down pinot grigio you now find on the market? Why not a vernaccia or a verdicchio with your next seafood meal instead of pinot grigio? Why not a French Pouilly-Fumé instead of that way-too-over-grassy New Zealand sauvignon blanc? Switzerland makes a white wine called ferdant that is ideal with veal, chicken or fish. Ferdant is a charming Swiss grape that makes a subtle medium-bodied white wine, stressed Liam to Lynch who couldn't help notice that Liam was becoming more interested than ever in wine.

—Learning about grapes and wine never ends. That's what the young Professor O'Malony had said. That's why the study and enjoyment of wine is so interesting; it begins all over with each new vintage, interrupted Gabriel.

—Almost every time I am at a wine tasting, I learn something new. Very recently, I tasted Turkish sparkling wine made from the narince grape. I'd never heard of it, Liam preached. I also had the still narince and then a blend of the narince and emir, all of which came from Turkey. The Anatolian wines from Kavaklidere make a Prestige Series, which included a red wine made from the öküzgözü grape. Never heard of it? Neither did I. It's gamay-like with a strong fruity nose but has a very dry earthy finish. It comes from the Elazig region of Turkey. The white narince wine I already mentioned has nice fruit up front but an almost soapy finish that Turkish food would, I assume, dissipate. The grape is grown in the Middle Anatolian region as well as in the Tokat region with the first being a bit rounder and showing more mouth-feel than the latter, Liam continued. I had to look it all up after I got back home, he said.

Each thought about continuing to learn more to enjoy more. Each contemplated that you stop growing when you stop learning and that every stoppage ends with death. As much as they enjoyed these round-table discussions, the same they had with their dead young professor, they often-times feared the knowledge they might learn. With great wisdom, he had told them, comes great sorrow.

Kavaklidere makes a blended red wine made from alicante and carignan. These grapes are also grown in America and France. The company adds wine made from öküzgözü and bogazkere grapes, which have been grown for centuries in Turkey, but the students still had a lot to learn about living better and coming to understand their own convictions about most things in life. Sean wanted to write or be a pilot using both professions to help flee the earth's reality and Gabriel wanted to direct movies. Both were artistic. Liam was still a lad who was excited by everything new he learned and Lynch had no idea what he wanted to do. Stephen, being older, had already failed at a few jobs and even a few university courses, but his Parnell-like personality demanded that the others pay respect.

—Remember the first time you had blue cheese spread on a fresh half fig, Gab? Well, that's how wine lovers feel about finding new wine grapes from areas not on everyday wine lists. The menu cheese and the menu wine are both exciting new taste adventures when paired correctly. Hard troublesome times can be eased a bit by making inexpensive new culinary and wine journeys. Gabriel listened closely to Sean Icarus as he continued. We're each an artificer of our own taste so we must take the time to enrich our sensual abilities. Not understanding our own sense of taste or smell makes our life a labyrinth of confusion.

—I talked about the Italian sparkling wine, Prosecco, over six years ago and now it is nearly the top selling sparkling wine in Dublin. Excellent examples can be found in every county, even in the Northwest of Ireland. It was people like you who were willing to try something new that created the influx of prosecco wines. The Bruts are very good but the Extra Dries are mostly cloying with a bit too much sugar left in them I think. It's a grape, a place and a style of sparkling wine you know. Spanish CAVA Brut is another sparkling wine perfectly suited to these hard times and they pleasantly cost very little. Reginato, in Argentina, makes a sparkling wine from chardonnay and torrontés with a delightful white grapefruit taste. Perfect before a meal. If you've had way too many chardonnays and merlots, there's a world of wines just waiting to be sampled, Stephen said. He was, after all, older and even Sean listened to his suggestions whenever he talked about wine. He, however, ignored almost everything else he talked about.

—The liquid part of the meal should change as often as you change your desire for different foods. This usually happens at the change of seasons like now and sometimes at mid-season. It took years to get people off merlot with every meal. Wine lovers sought out syrah and then grenache and are presently seeking wines made with the mouvrède grape. Some long-time wine drinkers even pair marsanne with hearty autumn chicken and veal dishes instead of chardonnay or the Ale their less-educated friends might drink, lectured Liam.

—And what else? asked Sean.

—Still, if you're adventurous, you'll look for big whites made with the clarette and bourboulenc grapes with some marsanne added. They can come from Lodi in the American state of California or their original home areas in France. Don't forget red wines made from carignan which usually have some cinsault added to them. There are so many unique grapes in the world and so many foods to match each of them with that you can be on a continuous culinary journey, continued Liam with a smile on his face and in his voice.

—Just a month ago I tasted a Terra Amata Rosé from the Cotes de Provence region in France which was made with geranche, cinsault, syrah, mourvedre, carignan, rolle and ugni blanc. It was a great dry wine, a copper-colored food-wine perfect for shrimp cocktail! I found it in the shop just past Trinity, said Gabriel whose family was now also into wine as a sign of better living which, sadly, they used for status.

—The ugni blanc, by the way, is one of the grapes that makes cognac, Sean said. He loved the idea that wine was a never ending study, a symbol of civilization, and a topic in which he excelled. He knew it would help his friends to also expand their view of the world and soar above the mundane as he did through pictures and books on the topic.

—I didn't know that.

—Last night I was sipping an Italian wine made with the cortese grape, and you too can begin to experiment with many new wines if you're willing to be open to trying something different, Lynch. Once you begin sampling new wines, and drink less Guinness, you'll start asking about how the wines were made and begin to look for wines made from the same grape but aged in different oaks. Even different coopers provide different flavor-notes by how they make their barrels, added Liam.

—Begin this weekend. Be different. Try a new restaurant when you get home to join your family for the holiday and also order some different food. Then, match it to a wine you've never had before. Start with some bubbles, I'd say, maybe a white with the appetizer and a winter-hardy red for the entrée. If you see me in the same place, send over a glass and I'll share whatever dessert wine I have, Sean answered with a pedantic tone of voice.

Before they left, the conversation changed to the new girl Lynch had been wanting to take out on a date and another girl, an American exchange student, who told Stephen that her family always had wine with meals ever since they had visited the famous Napa Valley. Stephen thought the American girl knew more than he did about most things and decided to not ask her out next semester. They were able to stop all discussion about the sadness they all took away from yesterday's Wake. They discussed nothing about the dead professor, instead, talked only about what they had learned from him.

*   *   *

Even the spirit of Boxing Day, which was coming soon, could not take away the gray dreariness of an overcast Dublin sky early in the early winter's evening. Sean was the first to restart the conversation they all participated in during their lunch break. Ever since the professor's Wake, they all felt the need to talk more, to look beyond what they could easily see and to seek out ways to follow his advice.

—Our taste and our attitudes change, as the weather grows colder. It's both psychological and physical science. Winter approaches and we look forward to wines and meals that make us comfortable. I have to go back to Waterford and I won't see any of you until next semester, but I wish I were flying to Spain or Italy, Sean stated, as he rearranged his topcoat over the back of his chair.

—For some years, Gabriel answered, I used to buy "futures", you know, that's paying for Bordeaux wines a year or two before they're released, and I'd save money because upon their release, they would always cost more. However, as French Bordeaux prices became unaffordable for me, I had to wait until the second winter or early spring after a vintage was released to buy some and even then I could only get a bottle or two. Now, I can't even afford a single bottle of any top Bordeaux. *Chateau Latour* will be

€2,000 a bottle; *Chateau Margaux* about the same: €24,000 a case! Even lesser Bordeaux will cost in the hundreds of Euros. It's so bad that some wine magazines have decided not to review the 2009 Bordeaux saying that since so few people can afford them, it's a waste of time to review them. Wealthy *Label Drinkers,* you know, people who don't really know what's good or bad, they just buy and show off the famous labels, will buy them. I find no comfort in that.

—So, what can I do to be comfortable with my wine tasting as cold weather sets in and I still want good wines with my winter meals? asked Liam. I know I'll have to seek out other wines and look to lesser-known grapes from around the world. Bordeaux is made with cabernet sauvignon and merlot with some cabernet franc. A few Bordeaux still include malbec and petit verdot. I can look for California wines made from the same grapes even though many California wines are much too "jammy" to pair with refined dishes.

I can look to South America where malbec has really blossomed or to Spain or Portugal where there are dozens of little known grapes that make food-friendly big red wines and citrus-mineral flavored whites for seafood or chicken on wet or snowy evenings. Right?

—That's what I'm doing, Gabriel said. Italy also makes a lot of little known reds. I had a legrein made by Alois Lageder not more than a week ago. The best Bordeaux are all out of my reach now so I look to Italy or Spain.

—Washington State in America makes merlot in a European style and Oregon, I'm told, makes some pinot noir in a true Burgundy style. New Zealand and Australia are also making some pinot noir and a few viognier wines in the continental style designed to marry with food. Italy still has some affordable wines like the Castello Di Gabbiano Chianti Classico for around €14 and I've always loved the Monsanto Chianti. Not bad for the majority of wine drinkers who are looking for pleasant wines in the fifteen to twenty Euro range, answered Lynch, but Guinness is still the cheapest. Right, Stephen?

There was no verbal response from him. Just a smile.

—Simply put, smart wine drinkers will pass on the super expensive wines from now on and will seek out good quality samples in a price range that proves that wine *really* is food and an excellent bottle should never cost much more than the salmon or lamb you make for your dinner guests! That's a rule we can be comfortable with as the snow approaches, Sean retorted.

—So, our New Year's Resolutions should be to Drink Wisely. Look for good values and wines made with grapes you may not know. Don't be afraid of wines you have never heard of and don't know. For example, Portugal has a nice red food wine called Terras Del Rei, which means the "lands of the king", and it's made with aragonez, a grape seen more and more on Portuguese labels and also some trincadeira which provides the blackberry aromas and castelao for body and color. At 13 percent alcohol, it's a great food wine costing under €7. So what if it doesn't say cabernet sauvignon or merlot on the label? added Gabriel. The entire Doyle family loved it since I first brought it home.

—If you do resolve to drink wisely, you'll also be willing to try new grapes and wines from places you didn't even know grew grapes, Stephen added.

As the cold night set in and all five young men slowed

down from late-autumn's academic rush, they knew there are longer winter nights ahead during which they'd eat more slowly and savor more wines with family and friends. Resolved to live better by expanding their buying of good wines, looking for quality inside the bottle, and not paying attention to the famous labels outside the bottle was what they all were thinking. They also recalled looking at the folded hands and still face of the dead young professor at the Wake, but no one mentioned it out loud.

Like a flash of light, or a Champagne cork flying across your view, the idea of being concerned with what is inside a bottle of wine being far more important than the label on the outside of the bottle struck Gabriel and Liam at the same time. They knew Sean was already aware of this and so was Stephen. Lynch, they assumed, would never search the heavens of thought to seek this conclusion. He'll always just drink what others buy for him or whatever cost the least. Lynch never told them what he'd learned from their favorite professor. He never said to any of them that the professor told him, one afternoon, that when the time comes for a man to die, his last words are never, I wished I had worked more. No, it's always I wish I spent more time enjoying what I loved.

—Try some pure cabernet franc for a red or vermentino or verdejo for whites. Sample all the Greek wines and look for wines from Switzerland. Make yourself comfortable this winter with new selections from the world of wines, Liam told the fellows. I once had a Clos des Papes. It's white Chateauneuf-du-Pape made with all six of the legal grapes in the French appellation. There's grenache blanc, roussanne, picpoul, clairette, bourboulenc and picardin in it. Its taste was mineral and quinine, maybe a bit salty, but so unique I had to learn more about other wines made with these grapes. It was Sean who told me that I'd never be able to learn all the grapes available to make unique and interesting wines, but I'll try to learn them all.

Quietly, the snow began to softly fall on The University Common Hall, Parnell's grave, and on Dublin City as well as all across Ireland, France and Northern Italy blanketing the leafless vineyards and the grave of their young professor as they were about to sleep through the cold lengthened night. The five seekers of wisdom all became quiet before they had to travel home to families who never discussed such fascinating and important aspects of living.

Stephen rose and left the table first. Lynch wanted to know if any of the others wanted to go out for a Guinness and Gabriel Doyle shook hands with all and wished each a Happy Holiday.

—You look like a priest when he holds the host high, Stephen shouted across the room to Liam as he headed out the door and into the virgin snow.

—I think I'll learn more about wine, he answered. There's a lot more to it than you think. Isn't there, Sean? I'm glad we went to the Wake.

It will be a great holiday indeed, Sean thought to himself, at least for the living.

Wine Labels

Mused by Charlotte Perkins Gilman

Peeople like Carol and myself seldom get the chance to visit the most famous Chateaux in the world. Seldom do ordinary people get to see ancient cellars filled with bottles blanketed with mold that lives on the alcohol vapors or to see priceless collections of corkscrews dating back for centuries or even visit a library of rare wine books. So, when I came home to rest for the summer, I was certainly pleased that Carol had my room decorated with a few fresh flowers and all the wine labels I, and she, had collected during the years we've been drinking wine together.

We had some labels in small frames and others pasted to large pieces of backer-board. We even had a few single labels, special ones, showcased in elaborate frames.

I had wine labels from bottles that we drank together while we were first dating and naturally, labels from the wines that were served at our wedding.

I hate to talk about this. I just want to rest this summer. I was told not to do anything. Just rest. I simply want Carol to enjoy some new wines with me and then help me remove the labels. Nothing else. It's not work; I'm resting while I arrange and organize them.

I've gotten older. I didn't want to, but it happened. Carol says all I need to do is rest. "Eat less food, drink lots of water and rest," she says. "The wine labels can wait."

I listen, but I ignore her.

I thought I was resting throughout this entire past spring while I was working on the label collection. I shouldn't really call it *working*. I loved doing it. I *had* to do it. Framing some, pasting others into scrap books, and gluing less important labels, like cheap Australian Shiraz labels and California Chardonnay examples that have the words "cellared and bottled by" printed on them onto my bathroom door. I glued everyday. I was neat. I tried to vary the grape types but still had trouble keeping the Zinfandels from touching or overlapping the Cabernets. Carol says not to worry if Merlot labels touch Pinot Noir labels, but you and I know that that should not happen.

I don't like my room one bit.

If I had longer walls, I could paste up more labels.

I wanted to visit a winery this summer but Carol says we have to wait. So I found my framed Chateau Leoville Barton 1970 and tried to count the number of trees in front of the ink-sketched chateau. I counted eleven. I hope I'm right. The red numbers: one, nine, seven and zero really stand out but they block the French letters: *mis en bouteille au chateau*. I like APPELATION ST. JULIEN CONTRÔLÉE in all capital letters. Carol and I can no longer afford Chateau Leoville Barton. Who can?

I counted eighteen windows on the older Chateau Durfort-Vivens label. I think that Bordeaux from Margaux has the prettiest aromas. Their labels never smell like the wines. Corks smell like corks, nothing else.

My room is airy enough but it's not an open vineyard in Napa Valley. She says I need the air. I feel ungrateful.

Carol shouted to me a few days ago that I should walk

more. "Please, put those wine-label scrapbooks down for a while and let's take a walk." I didn't answer. "It's really nice outside and you've been home for nearly two weeks. Let's go outside." I didn't answer.

I looked at all the open space on the walls of my room.

I opened another cardboard box of wine labels. I put the Catena 2009 Malbec next to the Joseph Carr Cabernet Sauvignon. Both are rectangular. Both are black on white with a bit of red. Catena stresses in red the vintage and the grape. Carr's red stresses Napa Valley. Carr hides the vintage year. Why? Catena has a little pencil sketch making the standard print even more noticeable. I've decided Argentina beats California today. I get so frustrated when I have to search for the year the wine was made. Some people hide the date on the back. I can't use any of these labels. I get frustrated when I can't glue down the edges of a label evenly. I get frustrated when Carol wants me to walk. Look at all that open space on the wall behind my bed.

I *am* resting. Yes. I note that the Italian Monte Antico is also black and white with some red. Its red, or maybe you'd call it rusty red, is the sketch of the winery placed below the word *Toscana* and grape names: Sangiovese, Merlot and Cabernet Sauvignon, then the vintage year. I have to assume they're placed in the order of percentage of volume used to blend the wine from the most used to the least used. Who knows? Carol doesn't.

I hate label tricks. I hate "vinted by" and "cellared by" when I'm looking for "produced by." I've torn up labels that really lied to me. I once burned a label that wouldn't answer my questions about the wine. I really like, "grown, produced and bottled by" the most. You see it less and less.

I finished my black and white and red collection for the day. I laughed to myself thinking that newspapers are black and white and read. I have two spots left. I set the Calon-Segur Saint-Estephe Medoc in one of them. Maybe it shouldn't be here. It has lots of red. I like the French word *Récolte* printed in red above the 1978 vintage date. The heart-shaped design around the Chateau's name below the inking of the house and vineyards is what makes you love the label. I finished the page with the Nieto Bonarda from Mendoza. Bonarda is printed in red because the word sounds red. I almost put a Lenz Moser Grüner Veltliner from Austria in this group. It is all green on white with two smidges of red over the word Trocken.

Trocken sounds hard. Green sounds sweet but not as sweet as yellow can be.

Carol says a month has gone by and I haven't finished decorating my longest wall with my wine labels. They are each separate areas of pictures or scenes. Together, they make an entirely different picture. It's Gestalt but Carol doesn't notice that.

I don't eat much when I work with the labels. I have no appetite. It is depressing when Carol wants me to eat and when she tells me my suffering increases her nervousness.

By the end of summer, I had not only the longest wall all prettied-up with labels but also the adjacent wall. I finished seventeen scrapbooks and I noticed many new and different pictures each time the light of the day changed. I was thin. I rested. I was less angry when Carol shouted orders to me. I stopped staring outside during the mornings. I saw things I had never before seen in the labels.

Banfi labels made me feel Italian. I loved them. The Coat-of-Arms overlapping the sketch of the castle on the Poggio Alle Mura Brunello di Montalcino is simply beautiful. Carol and I once visited the Banfi Castello. I hadn't known stress then and was not always tired.

A knight holding, a sword and a flag in the center of the vineyards with the cloudy sky beyond on the regular Banfi Brunello di Montalcino label. I liked the regular Brunello better. Maybe because we shared it when Carol and I first drank it. I think Banfi wines smell orange, not like an orange, but the way the color orange smells.

Fonseca Porto LBV's smell blue and their 1977 vintage smells an amber-gold edged purple. Croft, Taylor-Fladgate and Fonseca all have black and white labels. I love it when they print "bottled in 2011" in white on a black label or when they print it in black on a white label. They do that for me.

This morning, the small pictures were the same but the over-all large one slowly moved into a new perspective.

I told Carol. She said to not look at them and suggested she might have to help me remove them.

I put some labels on the lamp-shade. Carol took the entire shade away and brought back a plain new one. "Fire!" she exclaimed. "Fire could start if the paper got too hot."

I knew she was right. I covered my top windowpane with the labels from France, Germany, and Italy and Spain's Juan Gil label went in the corner. The new view was better than the old view.

Carol said I was not getting enough rest. "Maybe," she suggested, "I should take you back to the doctor who would get you to rest."

I didn't think I was tired.

That afternoon I watched the wine labels slowly rearrange themselves into a farmland country scene along the Rhone River. The *Cotes* were all golden. I wondered if the labels worked out new designs all night while I slept. I wondered what I was missing. I wondered if I should replace some key labels with others to help them finish their design. I wondered if I should stay up at night to see what's gong on.

I stopped working with Guigal Cote-Rotie labels because my hand got too dirty from all the stony soil. Some hot stones burned my fingertips. This was the same weekend that I got my finger nipped by a critter that was sitting peacefully on a white label. I had all the labels I could find with animals on them and put them in two very strong new boxes.

I noticed quickly that kangaroos, koala bears, parrots, and Vietti insects could be dangerous. Vietti Arnesi, Barbera, Dolcetto d'Alba and Moscato d'Asti all had its own bug or thorn bush on the label. I think the bugs are attracted to the Moscato more than anything and since I think it's the best Moscato made, I have to put up with the bugs. I ate a bug once when I was a boy. It had a crunchy *frizzante* feel. It had no *dolce* taste. I don't eat many bugs anymore.

Today, I'd prefer an Arneis with bugs.

At night I heard the animals. In the mornings, I noticed that some birds had flown to different trees and some of the critters had taken up new locations on different labels. They made me angry. I told Carol they made me angry but not that they had moved. I knew she'd be upset if I told her the little Australian animals were moving on my labels. Every night now, she had me fastened still.

On the first of September, I would not let her into my room. As she took my wine-less breakfast away, I locked the door behind her. I climbed out of bed and embraced the beast on the labels. I avoided swords. I moved into the hillsides and ran down the rows of vines. I smelled the purple. I scratched my legs on the rose bushes at the end of the rows of grape vines. Carol shouted to open the door. She shouted louder and even screamed. I joined my designs. I became a new label with red print across my forehead and grapes below my lips. The red number 1944 shown through my chest.

"I'll get help!" screamed Carol. I continued to merge with my favorite spots in the world. I would never come out of my label collection again.

On Wine

Completely unlike Emerson

Ernest Hemingway, when describing what Robert Jordan drank in *For Whom the Bell Tolls* back in the 1930s, said, "The wine was good, tasting faintly resinous from the wineskin, but excellent, light, and clean on his tongue." We assume it was Spanish wine because of the novel's setting, but we have no details to pin it down and details greatly add to a wine lover's insights and enjoyment in both literature and in wine. Mention an area like Bordeaux or Napa and we wonder what was the specific wine and if a special wine is named, we wonder what was its vintage. However, we also enjoy just seeing the object of our affection being mentioned and wine, in general, has been written about for centuries. From Plato, "Wine is a remedy for the moroseness of old age," to moderns like Robert Mondavi, "Wine is the only natural beverage that feeds not only the body, but the soul..."

Wine lovers become enthralled when they read something that includes a reference to the product they enjoy so much. However, the more specific the reference is, the more it's appreciated. "Good wine is a good familiar creature if it be well used," says William Shakespeare in *Othello*, II.iii.315 and again in the Epilogue of *As You Like It,* "Good wine needs no bush."[1] Both quotes intrigue

---

1. Wine shops in the 16th century would display an ivy bush to show they had good wine.

the oenophile, but neither mentions a specific wine that you can recall or dream about tasting someday. Specific is terrific. It's a maxim to follow when considering verbs, locations and wines. (He staggered into the room) is far better writing than (he came into the room) and (the small cave north of Billings overlooking the Yellowstone River) is better than (the cave in the mountain) and (he slowly poured the 1961 Chateau Latour) is better than (he slowly poured the red wine). However, we still find any reference to wine in any poem, story, novel, song or movie as an added bit of pleasure in any artistic creation.

"The wine of life is drawn, and the mere lees is left this vault to brag of," *Macbeth*, II.iii.95-96, is another Shakespearean reference to wine as he uses it to help explain how the best part of life was drawn off leaving only vile sediment to represent Macbeth's integrity after he lowers himself to thoughts and acts of murder. Shakespeare has so many wine references that without some knowledge of wine, it's impossible to teach or, as students, fully appreciate his plays. Pope John XXIII said, "Men are like wine – some turn to vinegar, but the best improve with age." Thus, studying the wines named in a work helps us study the character.

Many comments on drinking can add humor or some thought-provoking concept to a poem or story but a specific wine lights up the literary passage and adds verisimilitude to the plot. Homer Simpson says, "Alcohol...the cause of and solution to all of life's problems." It's funny and meditative at the same time but when James Bond, in *Goldfinger*, says, "My dear girl, there are some things that just aren't done, such as drinking Dom Perignon 1953 above the temperature of 38 degrees Fahrenheit," the sincere wine-lover expands his or her depth of knowledge and enjoyment to a deeper level than the Homer Simpson fan who is working with mere generality. Another Bond example is heard in *From Russia with Love* when he says, "Red wine with fish – well, that should have told me something." The double agent, Grant, had just surprised Bond and we see the scriptwriter teaching us that we can tell things about a person by what he eats and drinks. A similar point is made by Charles Dickens in his *Pickwick Papers*, chapter 8, where we read, "It wasn't the wine," murmured Mr. Snodgrass, in a broken voice. "It was the salmon."

Again, we learn about wine from Shakespeare: "A cup of hot wine with not a drop of allaying Tiber in 't," *Coriolanus*, II.i.52, refers to a time when the Romans added water to their wines to help dilute them. Henry Aldrich, who lived between 1647 and 1710, wrote a poem about drink and said, "If all be true that I do think, there are five reasons we should drink: Good wine – a friend – or being dry – or lest we should be by and by – or any other reason why." Subtle humor? Yes, but without a specific wine reference, it's a mere pun with no epiphany for the wine-loving reader. It's in the same vein as Johann Heinrich Voss who lived between 1751 and 1826 and wrote, "Who does not love wine, women, and song remains a fool his whole life long." No doubt true, but still it's surface-level inspiration.

"What is better to sit at the end of the day and drink wine with friends, or substitutes for friends!" wrote James Joyce while Henry Fielding wrote, "Wine is a turncoat; first a friend and then an enemy," meaning you should not drink too much but Joyce meant wine can console you even if you're alone. In both cases, knowing a little about the pleasures of wine adds to your comprehension and expands your thinking. If either had mentioned a specific wine, it would have forced the reader to linger longer in thought about agreeing or disagreeing with the comment. Sometimes the general statement does work. Henry Wadsworth Longfellow wrote, "When you ask one friend to dine, give him your best wine! When you ask two, the second best will do!" Isn't it true that great discussion can keep its focus with two but at a wine and cheese party, few, if any, defining comments are made regarding the wines? When Andre Simon, in his "Commonsense of Wine" said, "Wine makes every meal an occasion, every table more elegant, every day more civilized," he, in a sense, edited Longfellow by proclaiming the power of any wine and pointed out that wine-lovers tend to be more civilized than the average person so no matter what level of wine quality you serve, you're still making life for you and everyone around you better.

Every reference to wine draws *les amis du vin* into a deeper concentration. When very specific, any friend of wine glows with enjoyment by simply knowing or having heard of the mentioned wine. For example, in a 1944 James Thurber cartoon, the caption reads, "It's a naive domestic Burgundy without any breeding, but I think you'll be amused by its presumption." Because it's narrowed down to a Burgundy wine, we gather more from it than if it just said "wine". In *The Devil's Dictionary*, 1911, Ambrose Bierce, a writer with Poe-like skills, defined a connoisseur with the following: "An old wine-bibber having been smashed in a railway collision, some wine was poured on his lips to revive him. 'Pauillac, 1873,' he murmured and died." Again, we are more enthralled with not only a wine reference, but with a specific French wine from Bordeaux. When W.C. Fields stated, "What contemptible scoundrel stole the cork from my lunch," we are amused but had he mentioned a Chassagne-Montrachet or even a Zeller Schwarz Katz, we would have been more intrigued!

Alexander Dumas stated, "Montrachet should be drunk on the knees with the head bare." Specific. The statement ignites contemplation on the quality of the wine. Voltaire wrote about talking with a Burgundy winemaker: "I serve your Beaune to all my friends, but your Volnay I keep for myself." Specific. We wonder if the Volnay is really that much better than the Beaune? "Nothing makes the future look so rosy as to contemplate it through a glass of Chambertin," said Napoleon Bonaparte. Specific. It makes us look beyond the Gevrey-Chambertin, the village wine produced in larger quantities, and want to seek out the specific Grand Cru wines like Le Chambertin or possibly a Chambertin Clos de Bèze, the ones Napoleon drank.

When we read Shakespeare's famous sherry comment, "If I had a thousand sons, the first human principle I would teach them should be, to forswear thin potations and to addict themselves to sack," we have to know that the English called sherry, sack and even though it's not completely specific, we like the importance of a specific Spanish wine being stressed. "Pale Sherry at a funeral, golden at a wedding, brown at any time," wrote Charles Tovey, and continued, "Let your humor and your Sherry both be dry." Excellent specific advice. The only way Martin Armstrong could be more specific would be to note a vintage year when he wrote, "Praise first the great Chateau Lafite, Latour, Margaux, then two scarce less than Haut-Brion and Ausone, then all those names well known of wines of all degrees."

Robert Louis Stevenson was as specific as he could be for the time: "Wine of California...inimitable fragrance and soft fire...and the wine is bottled poetry." Wine-lovers read his statement, think of a Californian wine they've had and envision it as poetry in a bottle. It works. It's simply magic that makes wine incite deeper meditation and unlike other beverages, forces us to think more deeply. "When wild with much thoughts, 'tis to wine I fly, to sober me," wrote Herman Melville. It's always been that way. Centuries before Christ, we find written in the *Babylonian Talmud*, "There is no gladness without wine." Thomas Jefferson said, "Good wine is a necessity of life for me." You can't say much more about wine after that, can you?

"And wine maketh glad the heart of man," Psalms 104:15.

Wine then, adds not only pleasure when drunk, savored, studied and shared, but pleasure is also derived when it's talked about, written about or when even simply seen mentioned. The more specific the reference is, the more intense is the pleasure and excitement for all sincerely dedicated wine-lovers. *In vino veritas.*

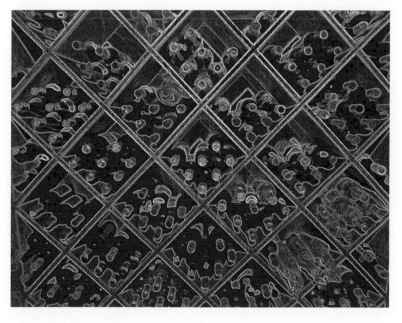

7/10

Photo by Paula Cella

John J. Mahoney is a Certified Wine Educator and a Literature Professor. He has judged wines across the United States and Europe, and has taught literature at high schools and colleges for over 40 years. He is Chancellor of the Dionysian Society International, a member of the American Wine Society, a *Chevalerie du Verre Galant* (Knights of Cognac), President of New Jersey Club Zinfandel, Director of the Tri-State Wine College, and is the voice of "Weekend Wine Tips" on the radio. He currently teaches British Literature for Seton Hall University at Saint Augustine Prep in Richland, New Jersey. He also hosts corporate wine education seminars and teaches wine classes each semester.